Martha and Mary of Bethany

Martha and Mary

of Bethany

A NOVEL

Gloria Howe Bremkamp

CARMEL • NEW YORK 10512

FIRST EDITION

This Guideposts edition is published by special arrangement with Harper-SanFrancisco.

*For MAP, whose friendship
is treasured and whose faith
is admired.*

1

MARY was the first to see the river and the crowd of people lining its banks. "Look! There must be hundreds of them!"

"That means we shall have a long wait, no doubt," said her sister, Martha, walking close beside her. She glanced over her shoulder toward her husband, Simon, and her brother, Lazarus. "I pray the rumors of John the Baptizer's healing powers are true."

"Many others join us in that hope," Lazarus said, pointing to those in the crowd being carried on litters or hobbling on canes or riding on donkeys as Simon was.

"He can't heal me," Simon said, a despairing certainty in his voice.

"We must let him try." Martha's tone was flat, uncontradictable.

"But what can a wilderness preacher do? Pray? The priests in Jerusalem have done that. And I'm not healed."

Martha stopped abruptly. "Nor do you believe you can be healed," she accused, emotion darkening her square-shaped face and deep-set eyes. "I sometimes think you do not want to be healed!"

"Don't say such a thing!" Mary told her sister.

"No one wants to be sick," said Lazarus. "And especially not with leprosy!"

"He's searching for healing. Even though the affliction is barely upon him," Mary added.

"I am not yet an outcast. You have not yet had to put me away in a leper's camp," Simon protested. "I came on this journey, didn't I? Am I not here?"

"Yes, physically you are here. But in your spirit you believe you can't be healed."

Simon gestured in disgust and resignation. "Have your own way. As always."

Martha turned and walked on. Like a thousand other Jewish women, she was of medium height and plump, the plumpness testifying to two things: the wealth of a household where food was always plentiful and her skills in supervising the family kitchen. Her hair was long and peppered with gray. She wore it loosely braided and wound about her head. It gave her a look of authority, and it suited her behavior.

For most of her thirty-five years she had been cast into the role of a woman of authority, having served as surrogate mother to Lazarus, three years her junior, and to Mary, who at age thirty was still the baby of the family. The role had been cast on her by their parents, accepted without protest by brother and sister, and thereafter acknowledged by relatives, friends, and neighbors.

She had never succeeded in throwing aside the role. She once confided to Simon that she found it to be a heavy burden. She could scarcely remember ever feeling young or reckless or free.

But then, freedom for a woman was an unattainable ideal anyway. What right had she even to hope for it? Men ruled. In government. In religion. In commerce. Even in the home women were not considered good enough to sit at the same table with their own men.

Only death made them equal or better. Then, as survivors of wealthy parents or husbands, as she was, women sometimes found themselves rewarded with property or goods. But even that status came about because they were considered inferior and incapable of earning their own livelihood. It was a strange role for death to play, she thought. It was as if death could somehow generate new life. How odd. Death was death. There was nothing after it. Nothing beyond. She had learned that with the death of her first husband. How odd, indeed. And how foolish of her to think on such things.

Especially at a time like this, when getting her present husband healed was so important. She could scarcely think of anything else. He must be healed. If she could will it, healing would already be his. Yet Simon's illness was out of her control. His healing was something she could not make a reality by an act of her own will. Still, she agonized for his healing. It must happen. She doubted she could survive being a widow a second time. Healing for Simon must be found!

If only he would believe it could happen!

"There is a good place to stop, Martha," Simon called out, pointing to a clump of willows beyond the road. "The shade will be most welcome. I am tired!"

She stepped off the roadway and led the family toward an unoccupied patch of shade along the river.

"Aren't you tired, too, Martha?" Simon asked.

"We all are," she replied, turning to help him down

from the donkey while Lazarus tethered the little animal. They had left their home in Bethany before the first faint blush of dawn on the journey to find John the Baptizer. They had followed the Jericho road through the wilderness of Judea, rested at noontide near Elisha's Spring, and now, finally at the river's edge, the day's ninth hour approached. "Wouldn't you be cooler if you unwound that head cover?" she asked, helping Simon to settle against one of the willows.

"I want no one to see me."

She understood. The sores on his face were spreading, wasting away the skin, destroying his features. She patted his bandaged hand and moved away to find a resting place for herself.

As she settled back against one of the willows, she realized how shallow the waters of the river were. At the fording place they barely reached a person's ankles. On either side of it they were a little deeper, but still reached only to a person's waist. It was in these deeper places where the Baptizer and three of his disciples stood midstream, calling for repentance from the crowd and blessing and baptizing all who responded.

Mary came toward her, took off her head shawl, spread it on the ground near her, and sat down. Lazarus squatted on his heels near Simon. The four of them sat in silence, glad to be resting, watching and listening to the crowd. In spite of its size it was surprisingly quiet. There was something respectful, almost reverential, about the crowd, as if an expectancy of hope abided in each person.

Some family groups spoke in low tones. Others simply watched the baptisms. Those who were lame waited patiently, taking their turns as strong-bodied family members helped them into the waters. A group of Pharisees stood apart from all the others. They wore phylacteries in a public show of prayerfulness. But they were not praying. They whispered among themselves and pointed toward the activities.

Of the four men administering the baptisms, it was easy to know which was John and which his disciples, Mary decided. Even though all of them were bearded, only one had the careless, unkempt look of a person dwelling in the wilderness, as she had been told John did. She'd also been told he often visited with the Essenes, that solitary group of mystics who lived south of Jericho on the shore of the Dead Sea. She wondered if the other three were from that group.

"Is John the Baptizer an Essene?" she asked.

"I think not," Martha replied. "He seems too separate, too apart."

"I, too, think he is a man alone," Lazarus said. "It is as written by the prophet Isaiah, 'He has the voice of one crying in the wilderness.'"

The Baptizer's face was tanned and weathered. His clothing was rough camel's hair, and around his waist he wore a leather girdle.

"He is rough looking, it's true," Mary said. "I wonder if it's also true that he eats locusts."

Martha scoffed. "More likely it is the fruit of the almond trees that he eats."

Mary protested. "But nearly everyone says he eats the insects."

"Nonsense!" Martha insisted. "It has to be the fruit of the almond tree. Like those in our own garden."

"Either way, locusts the insects or almonds—they do look similar—the Baptizer appears to be a strong man," Lazarus said.

The Baptizer once again repeated in a loud voice, "Repent! The kingdom of God is at hand!"

"He sounds like a fanatic to me," said Simon.

"If he can heal you, what does it matter?" Martha's voice held a sharp tone.

Mary leaned back against the willow, wishing that Martha would not be so sharp with Simon. Wanting to admonish her, she glanced toward her sister, but Martha had closed her eyes. Lazarus stretched out full length on the ground just beyond Simon. Both men seemed to be about to doze off. The trip had been harder on all of them than expected. She felt weary herself. And she shouldn't feel it like the others. She was the youngest, after all, and slender. The trip should have been easier on her, except for the sun and the heat. Because of her light complexion and hair, sun and heat always bothered her. She touched her face with tentative fingers. It felt very hot, and she looked again at Simon, closely wrapped to hide his affliction. How could he stand the heat she wondered, as a pang of sympathy went through her.

Often she was uncertain of her feelings about Simon. He was a gruff man but had great talent as a silversmith. He was the craftsman, whereas Lazarus was more the artist. They were well matched as business partners. Whenever the subject of Mary's mixed feelings about Simon came under discussion, Lazarus was always quick to reassure her that Simon was a man of integrity and sincerity.

"And he loves our sister," Lazarus would say. "Never

forget. It was Simon who saved Martha from the disgrace of early widowhood after Phares was killed."

It was true. And she supposed that in his gruff, blunt way, Simon really did love Martha. Sometimes it was hard to tell. But then sometimes it was hard to tell just how much Martha loved Simon. Lazarus said the marriage was a good one. She supposed he was right. Only a gruff, blunt man like Simon could stand up to Martha's bossiness.

Lazarus stood up to it by teasing Martha, by making her laugh, and then going on about his business regardless of what she thought. Mary wished she could stand up to Martha's bossiness like that. But somehow it seemed disloyal to do so. After all, Martha practically raised them both. Even when their parents were still living, Martha was the boss.

So far as a husband for herself was concerned, she had long since given up hope of finding anyone she could love enough to marry. She supposed she still grieved for Eban. Years had passed, and still she dreamed of him. She'd never met anyone else with the combination of gentleness and strength, decisiveness and thoughtfulness that he had.

After his father sent Eban off to marry the daughter of a rich merchant in Damascus, Lazarus and Simon tried to help find another suitable young man for her and invited several of their Jerusalem business acquaintances to the house. But she felt comfortable with none of them, and soon Lazarus and Simon despaired of finding someone for her.

Now that she was thirty, few men were interested even in meeting her. Those who might want a woman that old were either too old themselves or too crude. And so she had settled into the comfortable, protected routine of being the unmarried younger sister in the household.

Someday the emptiness left in her heart by the loss of Eban would be filled, she supposed. She hoped it would happen, somehow. She often prayed it would happen.

The droning of the Baptizer's voice continued. She shifted around to find a more comfortable position and thought how consoling it was that Lazarus had not yet married, either. Of course, the question of marriage was different for a man. It didn't seem to matter so much whether or not a man married.

And in her brother's case, he was always busy designing fine jewelry, working with the cutting and polishing of precious gems, or working with Simon on creating magnificent plates, bowls, platters, pitchers, and urns of silver and brass. Several artisans and craftsmen worked for them. The Tetrarch Herod Antipas was a frequent customer of their shop in the Jerusalem bazaar, and they did a brisk business repairing breastplates and helmets for the Roman officers stationed in Jerusalem.

Lazarus had no time for a wife, just as she no longer really had the time to give to a husband. What man would want a wife given to long walks alone, or to hiding in a corner of the house or garden with her sewing in order to meditate and to contemplate the meaning of life?

A breeze began, gently, in small puffs. Clouds began to drift across the stand of willows and the river, making patches in the sunlight and making the air seem cooler. Almost at the same moment the crowd began to murmur more loudly and stir about.

Mary straightened.

Martha opened her eyes and sat up.

"What is it?" Lazarus asked, getting up.

"Someone important is coming," Martha replied. "The crowd is giving way for him, making way for him."

"Perhaps it is Herod Antipas," Mary said with a laugh at her own sense of political humor.

Lazarus grinned and winked at her.

Everyone knew of the growing enmity between Herod and the Baptizer. Herod had divorced his wife and married the wife of his brother Philip. The Baptizer had publicly denounced the acts, calling them sins against the laws of God and the customs of man.

Martha missed the intended humor. "Herod would be the last person on earth to repent, let alone to come to the prophet for absolution."

"Speak quietly, woman, when you talk against Herod," Simon warned. "He is powerful. And he is a valued customer of our humble shop. We dare not offend him."

"Can you see who it is?" Mary asked.

Lazarus stood on tiptoe, trying to see over the heads of the crowd. "It's that group of Pharisees. They're moving toward the water now. Can you see them?"

"The Baptizer has certainly seen them," Martha pointed. "Look at his reaction to them!"

From midstream the Baptizer faced the approaching Pharisees, his face dark with disapproval.

"And hear his words . . ."

"O generation of vipers, who has warned you to flee from the wrath to come? Pride in your religious rituals will not save you. You cannot fool God."

They strained unsuccessfully to hear the response of the Pharisees.

John's voice continued to come clearly to them all.

"I indeed baptize you with water unto repentance: but he that comes after me is mightier than I. He shall baptize you with the Holy Ghost, and with fire!"

Mary and Martha exchanged a puzzled look.

"Who is that? Who is he talking about?" Simon asked.

Lazarus shook his head.

"Whoever he means," Martha said, "the Pharisees are disturbed and are retreating."

"You're right," Lazarus said. "They're turning back away from the river."

Muttering and laughing, the crowd made way for them to pass through and depart.

The Baptizer waded back into midstream, once more calling out for all to hear, "Repent! The kingdom of God is at hand!" Many from the crowd responded. Some now carried their crippled and sick relatives with them to the middle of the stream. Many others seated themselves along the river's edge, tired from standing so long. The breeze stirred fitfully at the afternoon's heat, and clouds played a game of hide-and-seek with the sun.

"We should take you to the Baptizer now, Simon, my husband. Are you ready?"

Simon nodded.

Lazarus helped him onto his feet.

Suddenly a new kind of murmuring began in the crowd.

Simon and Lazarus turned to watch as a tall, dark-haired man stepped from the midst of the crowd and moved toward the water's edge.

The Baptizer looked directly at the man, glanced away, and then looked back at him, this time staring in astonished recognition. He bowed, and when he once again straightened, there was a look of reverence on his face.

The man spoke to him in a tone that none could clearly hear.

The Baptizer responded by raising his hands and shaking his head as if refusing to perform the ritual baptism for this supplicant.

The sun suddenly hid its face behind a cloud.

Something haunting and familiar stirred inside Mary. She moved away from her family and went toward the river's edge.

"Don't wander too far," Martha warned.

The words went unheard, so rapt was Mary's attention on the man now standing midstream with the Baptizer. They were about the same height. They even had something of the look of kinship about their features. They might be cousins, she thought unexpectedly. But where the Baptizer was rough and aggressive looking, the other man had an entirely different presence about him. It was a presence of authority. She kept looking at them both, trying to decide if that was the difference between them, trying also to name the qualities that would create such a response in her own heart at the mere sight of this stranger.

He was strong looking, but he seemed gentle somehow. He was handsome, but not too handsome. His features, much more regular than those of the Baptizer, could have belonged to a Roman or a Greek as easily as to a Jew. Above all else there was a presence of authority about him that touched some deep strand of understanding in her.

Why should she feel this way? Who was this man?

He spoke.

The Baptizer lowered his hands and gave a shrug. "It is I who have need to be baptized of you. How is it you have come to me?"

"Let it be so for now," the tall man said. "It is our duty to follow the law."

The Baptizer nodded.

The tall man knelt in front of him.

With cupped hands the Baptizer took water from the river and anointed the supplicant's head. "The kingdom of God is at hand," he said, lifting his eyes heavenward.

Sunlight, golden, pure, white, pushed aside the clouds and bathed the land with brilliance. The crowd murmured and fell back. But the lame reached upward as if to grasp some special healing from the light itself.

The tall man stood up.

The light from heaven grew even more brilliant.

Mary caught her breath, for in the brilliance she perceived the Spirit of God descending like a dove and lighting on the tall man. She trembled at the wonder of it, and the haunting, familiar feeling in her heart resolved itself into sure and reverent acceptance of the wonder that it was.

At that moment she heard the voice from heaven saying, "This is my beloved Son, in whom I am well pleased."

"Martha, look!" she exclaimed.

"Look? At what?"

Mary pointed at the dove.

"I don't see anything."

"But it's so beautiful."

"You dream too much."

"And you are too practical," Simon said. "Leave the girl alone to dream and see beauty as she will."

Martha turned, surprised at the rebuff. "Without practical people, the work of the world would not be done."

Ignoring her, Simon limped forward. "Come on, Lazarus, help me to the river."

The Baptizer and the tall man waded up out of the water and bid each other farewell at the river's edge. The tall man walked away toward the south and west in the direction of the Dead Sea and wilderness of Judea. The Baptizer stood quietly, watching him go.

Martha brushed her way through the throng toward the Baptizer. "Your pardon, kind sir," she began.

He turned and looked at her.

"My husband is ill. My brother and sister and I have brought him here to have you pray for his healing. If you please, kind sir?"

Mary, with Simon and Lazarus, came up next to her.

"Will you pray for our brother?" Lazarus asked. "We have prayed in the great Temple in Jerusalem without success."

"We have offered special sacrifices," Mary added.

"But nothing has helped him," Martha said, fighting to hold back the tears that suddenly insisted on coming into her eyes. "Will you pray for his healing, sir?"

"Of course," the Baptizer quickly agreed. "I will pray for his healing. But it is the power of God that heals, not mine. Of myself, I have no power. None at all."

Martha wiped at her eyes.

"There is one who has the power of God for healing."

"And who is that?"

The Baptizer turned and pointed in the direction

where the tall man disappeared. "The man who just left here."

"You mean the man on whom the Spirit of love descended?" Mary asked.

Martha, Lazarus, and Simon looked at her in astonishment.

The Baptizer smiled at her. "Then you saw it, too?"

Feeling an unexplainable joy, she nodded.

The Baptizer turned again to Martha, Lazarus, and Simon. "Did you, also, see it?"

They shook their heads.

"That man is of God. He has the power to heal. I have only the power to pray for your solace and comfort. And to prepare the way for that man."

"But he has left!" Martha cried.

"We'll go and search for him," Lazarus said, trying to comfort her.

"Who did you say he was?" Mary asked.

"He is from Nazareth. His name is Jesus bar Joseph. Jesus of Nazareth."

"Jesus. Jesus of Nazareth," Martha repeated. "We must go and find this Jesus. For Simon's sake, for Simon's healing, we must find him."

2

THE stress of travel weighed heavily on all the family. But the disappointment of not being able to meet Jesus, and seek his healing powers, was even greater. Lazarus had gone in the direction the Baptizer pointed out, hoping to catch up with Jesus. He was unsuccessful. It was as if Jesus had vanished, spirited away by some unseen force.

The family returned to Bethany the next day and sent out two of their servants to search for Jesus. The servants journeyed many miles and were gone many days inquiring of other travelers. They stopped every householder, every shepherd. They even asked those people who restlessly roamed the wild places with their tents and herds. No one knew of such a person as Jesus of Nazareth.

Dejected and more sure than ever that it was his fate not to be healed, Simon secluded himself in the garden beyond the courtyard. Martha, worried and upset by his attitude, found no pleasure in resuming command of the household. Mary tried to help her as much as she could, but her thoughts were much on the man named Jesus and what she had seen and heard at the time of his baptism. Lazarus went back to work in the shop he and Simon owned in Jerusalem's bazaar.

On the third day after his return, an uproar outside the shop drew his attention. He went to the entrance and looked out into the street where two Temple guards were beating a third man and shouting obscenities at him.

"What has he done?" Lazarus asked Bulla, the most trusted of his artisans, who had also come out of the shop to observe the fracas.

"They think that man is a Zealot."

"A Zealot? That poor wretch?"

Bulla nodded. "You would think a Temple guard would know better."

"What do you mean?"

"The man is a beggar. And a blind one at that! He is often here in the Street of Silversmiths."

"A blind beggar? Then we must help him." He started forward.

Bulla grabbed the sleeve of his tunic, stopping him. "No, Lazarus! Why involve yourself?"

"But the man needs help!" he exclaimed, surprised and angered by Bulla's attitude.

"It is dangerous to interfere."

He jerked loose from Bulla's grasp and moved to help the man. But before he could reach him, a shout came from the other end of the street.

The Temple guards hesitated, looked up, and saw Roman soldiers hurrying toward them. They let go of their victim and shoved him away.

He stumbled and staggered, trying not to fall.

Lazarus rushed forward, caught him, lowered him onto the cobbles of the street, and knelt beside him. The man's face was bloody. His eyes were closed. His body shuddered with fear and pain, and then abruptly was as still as the stones he rested on.

All except one of the Roman soldiers rushed past, chasing after the Temple guards. The Roman who stopped knelt down, inspected the victim, then glanced at Lazarus. "What do you know of this man?"

"He was being beaten. He needed help."

"He is a blind beggar," Bulla said, coming up to them. "He often was here in the Street of Silversmiths."

"Why did they beat him?" the Roman asked.

"They thought him to be a Zealot."

"We don't know that, Bulla. You assume it," Lazarus said, getting to his feet.

"What other reason would they have?" Bulla insisted.

The Roman soldier also stood up and looked at Lazarus in a probing way. "Were you a friend of this beggar?"

Lazarus shook his head. "He was just a man who needed help."

"I told him not to get involved," Bulla quickly explained, as if deputized as a defender.

"And why would you do that?" the Roman asked.

Bulla looked surprised.

"Why would you not want him to get involved?" the Roman asked again.

"I didn't want him to get hurt. He is a great artisan. I work for him. This is his shop. He is Lazarus, the silversmith."

The expression of the Roman's face altered at the mention of the name Lazarus. He turned. "You are the man I was on my way to see."

Lazarus looked more carefully at the Roman. He was about the same height and build as himself, and about the same age, too, he guessed. He had a firm jaw and a strong brow. His eyes were blue, like the blue of a winter sky, and they held a look of directness and openness that Lazarus liked. This was a man who could be trusted, he thought, even though he was a Roman. "Why were you on your way to find me?"

"To bring you a message from the Tetrarch Herod Antipas."

"You, a Roman, carrying a message from Herod?"

The man laughed in an agreeable way. "I am the liaison officer assigned to Herod Antipas by the Roman garrison here in Jerusalem. My name is Delos Marcus. I am a centurion assigned to run Herod's more important errands when he doesn't want members of his own court to know anything about them."

"And what is he keeping from them now?"

The Roman glanced at the crowd gathering to look at the dead beggar. "Inside your shop might be a better place to talk, silversmith."

Lazarus called two other men who worked for him to come and stand watch with Bulla over the dead beggar until the other Roman soldiers came back. Then he went inside the shop. The Roman officer followed. "Now, tell me how I can be of help to Herod . . . and to you, as well."

"The Tetrarch is now in his palace at Jericho," Delos Marcus explained. "He wants you to come to him, and you are to bring as many baubles as you have in your shop for the pleasure of his new wife, the Lady Herodias."

"Ahhh . . ." Lazarus sat down on the rough wooden bench near the doorway, watching the crowd gather around the dead beggar.

"You don't seem surprised at receiving a summons from Herod Antipas," Delos Marcus said, looking about the shop. Finely wrought utensils of silver, bronze, copper, and gold were displayed on shelves. Beneath them, in wooden boxes, was an array of uncut gemstones. Toward the back of the shop, four craftsmen worked, and beyond them, near the shop's rear exit, barely visible through a beaded curtain, were the fires and crucibles necessary to metalworking.

"I am not surprised at Herod's summons," Lazarus confirmed. "His Excellency seems to need jewels often for the Lady Herodias. And I am most pleased that he buys from this shop."

"It means good business for you since his new wife is so demanding."

"Some women prefer more jewels than others," Lazarus said carefully.

The Roman laughed. "It seems the Lady Herodias prefers more of everything than most women do. It is well known that she demands more of Antipas than his first wife ever did."

Lazarus shrugged, unwilling to share gossip further with this Roman he had just met. Though he seemed trustworthy, one still should be careful. These were times when a careless word could bring trouble from the authorities.

"I hear the Lady Herodias is even demanding the arrest and imprisonment of that wilderness preacher," Delos Marcus went on. "The man they call John the Baptizer."

Lazarus glanced at him in surprise. "Why?"

"She claims the preacher has insulted her."

"Oh?"

"He is proclaiming that her marriage to Antipas is a sin against your God, and against your Jewish customs."

Lazarus got up and walked to the entrance of the shop. The Roman soldiers had returned with the runaway Temple guards and were ordering them to carry the dead beggar outside the city for burial in a potter's field.

There was no actual connection between the news he had just heard and the dead beggar. And yet, somehow, in the depths of his spirit, he sensed that there was. The stress of the times made it dangerous to think differently, to express a divergent opinion, to behave in a way not approved of by the Sanhedrin or the priesthood or the Romans or by the tetrarch and his lady. A strand of injustice and cruelty made the connection between the two events. It was a worrisome connection, and yet it was one about which he could do nothing. He turned again to Delos Marcus. "How soon am I to leave for Jericho?"

"Can you be ready by dawn tomorrow?"

He nodded.

"Good. I am instructed to accompany you with my squad of legionnaires, and . . ." He hesitated, laughing at the look of surprise crossing Lazarus's face. "Herod Antipas fears for the safety of the jewels you will be carrying," he explained. "Nothing more, I assure you, silversmith!"

The palace at Jericho was built by Herod Antipas's father, Herod the Great. Antipas had been only a small boy at the time. Now in his manhood he considered it one of his favorite properties. Certainly it was one of the most beautiful of all the Herodian buildings because of its location in the deep rift of the Jordan Valley. Always warmer than many other parts of Judea, the valley nurtured flowers, shrubs, and trees in great abundance. Forests of balsam palms, from which was harvested the sugary serum for balsam rum, lavished the Plain of Jericho with greenness and shade. Date palms, almond, olive, and orange trees grew in random profusion. Pomegranate, oleander, and cyclamen splashed their colors everywhere in between. All were evidence of the generosity of deep natural springs that had sustained life in Jericho for more generations than Lazarus could imagine.

On his arrival at the palace, he, Bulla, and their wares were ushered immediately into the private apartment of Herod Antipas. The centurion Delos Marcus, however, was noticeably excluded.

"It is good you have come so quickly, silversmith," the tetrarch said, walking toward him. His swarthy face creased into an uncharacteristic smile.

Lazarus and Bulla both bowed.

Lazarus straightened. "It is a great honor to have been summoned, your Excellency."

Bulla went to a nearby table, opened the baskets and boxes filled with samples of the shop's wares, and began to pull out some of the more unusual items—carnelian earrings, necklaces of gold and lapis lazuli, bracelets of onyx, coral, and turquoise, a magnificent golden salver embossed with intertwining acanthus and pomegranate, and an equally beautiful silver pitcher with matching cups and tray.

Lazarus pointed to the display. "How can we help you, my lord?"

Antipas walked to the table and examined the wares briefly, then turned. "There is nothing here that is suitable."

Bulla stopped and glanced around in surprise.

Lazarus cautioned him with a quick look.

The tetrarch fingered some of the jewelry. "I need something very special, silversmith."

"My lord?"

"A crown."

"A crown?"

The tetrarch nodded. "For my wife. The Lady Herodias must have a crown!"

Lazarus could feel Bulla's astonished stare on the back of his neck, and he hoped that his own astonishment was not apparent. Roman law prohibited local rulers from wearing crowns. Only the emperor himself was allowed this particular symbol of office. Romans took the law seriously. In fact, Romans were as serious about this particular law as Jews were about their law prohibiting the use of statues in their synagogues. Lazarus looked probingly at Herod Antipas, wondering if the request was some test of loyalty or some prank of humor.

But the expression on the tetrarch's face was one of genuine sincerity. He came close and said in a confidential tone, "You see, my friend, my first wife, if you will recall, is of the royal house of Nabatea. She is a princess. And as important as my first wife was to me, for a time, the Lady Herodias is even more important. I wish the Lady Herodias to know that I consider her even more than a royal princess. I wish her to know that I consider her a royal queen in every respect!"

Madness, Lazarus thought.

"I wish you to design the most beautiful crown ever to be designed. For her."

Madness. Sheer madness. It could be nothing else.

"Can you do it?"

"Do it?"

"Yes. Can you make such a crown?"

"Of course. But, my lord, the Roman law . . ."

Herod Antipas gave a gesture dismissing the importance of the reminder. "I have not forgotten the Roman law. I am too much of a Roman in my own thinking to forget it. But in Perea, at the Fortress Machaerus, the Lady Herodias will be safe in wearing it. Only there will she wear it. The Romans need never know. I never invite them to Machaerus. Now I say again, can you create such a crown for me?"

Unconvinced by the tetrarch's argument, but also recognizing that loss of business by default was foolish, Lazarus agreed to design a crown for the Lady Herodias.

Herod smiled in satisfaction and turned again to the items Lazarus and Bulla had brought with them. "I will buy all of these, as well," Herod said, and he thrust a bag of gold coins into Lazarus's startled hands.

The next morning Lazarus departed from the royal palace in Jericho, leaving Bulla to measure the head of the Lady Herodias so that the crown would fit perfectly and to adjust to size all the other jewelry the tetrarch had purchased. It was a sizable sale.

He felt of the bag of gold coins inside his tunic and smiled. Simon would be pleased, he thought. The price of the crown would have to be figured later when a design had been decided upon. But even now he knew that the price would be more than enough to hire another craftsman. That, too, would please Simon.

He walked steadily, not hurrying in the heat, though he was anxious to share the news of the sale with the family. He was equally anxious to learn if the servants had found the man Jesus. For better than two hours he walked. The heat became more fierce. It festered up off the rough road driven by a sultry wind.

By the time he reached the plateau halfway up the steep rise from the valley, he was breathless and his legs trembled from the exertion of the upward climb. There were no trees growing at this part of the roadway. There was no shade to rest in, no relief from the merciless sun, except for a rocky outcropping to the left of the road.

He made his way toward it and crawled into the meager shadow it cast. Someone else was already there. "Apologies! I did not see you," he exclaimed, starting to back out.

"No apology is needed," said the man already occupying the shelter. "Come, you're welcome to share this scant shade with me."

Lazarus hesitated, suddenly remembering the bag of gold he had hidden in the folds of his tunic and wondering if he was taking an unnecessary risk by seeking shelter with a stranger whose face he could not make out because of the sun's glare.

"There is room for you, too," the stranger said, moving to make more space available.

Risk or not, he needed respite from the sun. "You are kind." He crawled under the overhang and, with a sigh of relief, threw off his cloak. As he settled himself and his eyes gradually grew accustomed to the softer light of the shaded niche, he turned to look at the man beside him.

He was in a half-reclining position, his head resting against the back wall of the outcropping. He had his eyes closed, a fact that made Lazarus feel more at ease about studying him. His features were regular but marked with an uncommon strength even in profile. His beard was full, and his hair, dark in color, reached only to the nape of his neck in a style worn by many other men. Half-sitting, half-reclining side by side, as they were, Lazarus guessed the man to be as tall as himself. And he guessed their ages to be about the same.

He looked again at the man's face, feeling there was something familiar about it. Was he a customer of the shop in Jerusalem? Had he seen him at the palace in Jericho? Or had he been among the crowd at the River Jordan?

He straightened to look at the man more directly. Of course! The river! He had seen him at the river. He had not been in the crowd, though. And his face had worn no look of hunger, nor had it seemed so lined with fatigue as it was now. Could this be the same man? Could this be Jesus of Nazareth? Could this be the man with the power to heal?

If it was the same man, where had he been all the days they had searched for him? Where, indeed? This looked like a man who had been fasting far too long; one who had suffered, as if in a wilderness of doubt and temptation. Maybe this was not Jesus of Nazareth, after all. In spite of the curious presence of strength he had first noticed about Jesus, Lazarus felt this man looked nothing like a healer should look.

The man stirred, opened his eyes and smiled, seeming to take no offense at Lazarus' scrutiny of him.

From the folds of his cloak, Lazarus pulled forth a small packet of bread and cheese and offered it to him.

The man straightened. "Your generosity is most welcome." Carefully, he pulled apart the bread into two equal pieces and handed one back to Lazarus. He then did the same thing with the cheese.

Lazarus acknowledged the evenness of his action with a nod, pleased at his obvious fairness. But it was with respect and contrition that he acknowledged the man's next action.

It was a gesture of thanksgiving with the bread and cheese raised heavenward in grateful hands as he said, "From the bondage of death to the freedom of life, we praise your Holy Name, O God." Only then did he eat.

Lazarus did not. "You come from Nazareth, don't you?"

The man nodded.

"You are Jesus of Nazareth, aren't you?"

"How do you know me?"

"We saw you at your baptism. We have been searching for you ever since."

"We? Searching?"

Lazarus laid aside his bread and cheese. "The Baptizer told me and my sisters that you are a healer. My brother-in-law needs healing. We have been searching for you."

"It is the power of The Lord which you seek. I have no such power."

A sinking feeling went through him. Had he misunderstood the Baptizer? In the next instant, he was sure he had not, and he said, "But you have the right to exercise that power of healing. I have faith that you do."

An odd look filtered across Jesus' face.

It came and went so quickly that Lazarus wondered if he had really seen it, and if he had, what it meant.

In the next instant, Jesus was looking directly at him, probing his innermost being, testing the sincerity of his words.

"Will you journey with me to my home in Bethany?" Lazarus asked. "Will you come and visit with Simon?"

3

IT was Martha who first saw them coming up the road from the east. She stopped pruning an oleander bush, handed the pruning tool to Zoë, her most trusted household servant, and waved to the approaching pair.

"Who is it?" Simon asked from his secluded corner of the garden.

"Lazarus. It is Lazarus . . . and . . ."

"And? And? What does that mean?" Simon urged impatiently.

"It means there is someone with him."

"Bulla, most likely," Simon muttered.

"No . . . no," Martha countered. "This person does not walk like Bulla. He is younger. And from the looks of him, he is much stronger than Bulla." To see them better she moved away from the oleander and leaned against the rock wall defining the limits of the garden.

"Is it that Roman centurion?"

"No. This is no Roman walking with Lazarus."

Zoë came up beside her. "From his clothes he looks like one of us."

A groan of protest came from Simon. "Another one of Lazarus's friends who will stay forever and eat us out of house and home, I suppose."

"And what if it is?" Martha snapped, glancing toward Simon's hideaway. "This house has never turned away anyone. Nor is it ever likely to."

"Look, mistress," Zoë said, pointing now to the approaching pair. "The stranger wears a Galilean robe."

"Are you certain?" Martha asked in surprise.

Before Zoë could answer, Lazarus waved and called out, "Ho! Martha!"

"Can I believe my eyes?" she exclaimed, returning his greeting. Excitement began to course through her. "Can it be?"

"Who did you say it was?" Simon insisted. "Who is it with Lazarus?"

"You know him, mistress?"

"Who is it, Martha?" Simon demanded.

"It is Jesus. Jesus of Nazareth. The man we've been looking for. The man with the power to heal you, Simon!"

A heavy silence abruptly enveloped Simon's corner of the garden.

Martha turned to Zoë. "Go and tell the others that Lazarus has returned and has brought a very important guest with him. Tell the servants to prepare baths and food."

Zoë moved off and disappeared inside the house as Lazarus and Jesus came inside the gate.

"Martha, this is Jesus," Lazarus said. "He is the man that John the Baptizer told us about."

She appraised Jesus with a direct look, wondering what gave him the power to heal. He seemed ordinary, though there was an openness in his face that she found pleasant. His eyes held a reassuring look of calmness. But something stirred deep in her spirit, telling her that this was no ordinary man. There was something different about him—a presence, a dimension of character for which she could find no words.

"Jesus is on his way back to Galilee," Lazarus said. "I have invited him to break his journey here with us."

"You are doubly welcome in our home," she said, still appraising him. "You are welcome to rest and refresh yourself because my brother brings you here. And you are welcome, as well, for the blessing of healing that you bring for my husband."

He acknowledged her directness with a respectful nod. "I thank you for your hospitality. And your brother has already told me of your husband's need."

Mary appeared in the doorway of the house. At the sight of Jesus, a joyous radiance came over her face. She ran to them, gave Lazarus a welcoming hug, and then bowed to Jesus.

"And this is my sister, Mary," Lazarus said laughing. Beyond, inside the house, the servants peered out from doorways and windows. He laughed again and pointed to them. "In fact, the entire household bids you welcome!"

"Lazarus is quite right," Martha said. "The servants are preparing baths for you both, and food, too."

"A bath?" Jesus exclaimed. "That is more than hospitality calls for! A simple washing of the feet would be ample."

"Not for travelers as dusty as the two of you!" Martha quickly replied.

"We'd best do as she says," Lazarus grinned, "or she'll insist on bathing us herself!"

Jesus laughed and nodded acceptance.

"Where is Simon?" Lazarus asked, suddenly looking around.

Martha pointed to the garden retreat. "He is hiding."

"Does Simon know that Jesus is with me?" Lazarus asked.

"Yes. I think he does."

Brother and sister exchanged a knowing look. Then Lazarus shrugged. "Simon has much pride," he explained.

"And much embarrassment," Mary said softly.

"And much unbelief!" Martha added, giving Jesus another direct look.

He made no reply.

"But come," Martha continued, turning toward the house. "You both must bathe, rest, and let us feed you."

As they finished setting the table for the meal to come, Mary said, "He is different from other men, I think."

"Who? Our brother?" Martha asked in an overly solemn tone and with a straight face.

"Jesus is too important to tease about, my sister," Mary corrected. "He is a teacher, a rabboni."

"Does that mean he has no humor?"

Mary frowned at her. "You know what I mean."

Martha hesitated, realizing how much in awe of Jesus her sister was. She was a little in awe of him herself, in spite of her bold words. She went to Mary and put her arm around her shoulder. "Yes, I do know what you mean. There is a quality about him that makes him different. Maybe more different from any man who has ever been a guest in this house. But I can't explain this quality he has."

"I think I know what it is." Mary walked across the room and sat down on a small wooden bench.

Martha followed and sat beside her. "Tell me. What is it that makes this Jesus of Nazareth so different?"

"It's something I saw . . . and heard . . . at the river."

"At the river?"

"When he was baptized," Mary nodded.

"What did you see?"

Mary glanced at her shyly. "You won't laugh?"

Martha shook her head. "What was it you saw?"

"A dove."

"A dove?"

"A dove. It descended from heaven. It rested on his shoulder as he came up out of the river."

"I didn't see it."

"But I did." There was no shyness in Mary's voice now. "I saw the dove. And I heard a voice. A great and powerful voice that yet was proud and gentle. It was not like any voice I've ever heard before. It was like . . . like hearing . . . It was like hearing the voice of God."

Astonished, Martha straightened. Disbelief argued with reality. The voice of God? How could that be? And yet whatever else Mary was—a dreamer, sometimes lazy—she was not a liar. But the voice of God? "What did the voice say?" she asked very quietly.

Mary turned and looked at her. Tears of wonder at the memory were in her eyes.

"Well? What did the voice say?" Martha asked again.

"The voice said, 'This is my son, in whom I am well pleased.'"

"And these words referred to Jesus?"

Mary nodded and brushed at her tears.

Martha stared unseeingly about the room, trying to sort out the meaning of Mary's vision. Why hadn't she herself seen and heard what Mary had? She was as religious as Mary. Maybe even more religious than Mary, for she backed up her own faith with works. Mary often just sat and daydreamed. It was she, not Mary, not Lazarus, but she who first believed that Simon could be healed by prayer. She was the one who had the faith. Why hadn't she seen the dove descending? Why hadn't she heard the voice?

Before she could probe the questions, Lazarus and Jesus came into the room. They were freshly bathed and clad in new robes that she recognized as the ones Lazarus had only recently had made for himself. The new knowledge about what Mary saw and heard at Jesus' baptism pushed at her.

She now scrutinized Jesus' tall figure. He was well muscled and walked with a lithe grace. Like an athlete. He was a handsome man, she decided. There was an air of majesty about him. As well there should be if he was the Son of God, she thought. Maybe that explained the strange presence about him for which she still had no words. But did she dare believe it? How could she?

Jesus turned and smiled at her as if knowing what she searched for in her scrutiny.

Embarrassed that her thoughts should be so transparent, she stood up and started to leave the men to their meal. Mary rose to follow.

"Ask your sisters to share our food, Lazarus," Jesus said, seating himself at the big round table.

All three of them looked at him in surprise. Zoë and another of the household servants stiffened with shock. Women did not share meals with men. Surely Jesus knew that. As rough and provincial as Galileans were known to be, they still knew the custom of separating men and women at mealtime. It was a universal custom. Except for the Romans, of course. But then, Roman customs were different in many ways. For a Jewish household, however, to allow a mixture of men and women at the same table was as unheard of as mixing milk dishes and meat dishes in the serving of food.

Jesus gave a soft laugh. "Are there not enough things to separate us? A meal should be a time of sharing. Come. I want to know you better."

Mary glanced at Martha, hesitant and questioning. Martha and Lazarus exchanged looks of doubt.

"I have sisters of my own, Lazarus. Encourage yours to share this meal with us."

Lazarus straightened. "It is the rule of this house that a guest's request should be honored. If Jesus wishes you to share the meal, then you should."

Martha remained where she was, glancing from one to the other of them, still uncertain about what she should do. Mary waited to follow her lead.

"I have spent the past forty days in the wilderness," Jesus said. "I went there to fast and pray. I went there seeking to know what my Father would have me do."

Martha suddenly found her voice. "And what did this father of yours tell you?"

"He told me to teach people to love one another. To teach them to share with each other."

An unexpected lump rose in Martha's throat. She swallowed hard.

Mary's eyes instantly filled with tears.

Lazarus got up, went to his sisters, put his arms around both of them, and led them to the table.

Martha cleared her throat. "You are a breaker of barriers, Jesus of Nazareth."

He nodded. "And you are a plainspoken, practical

woman who will understand that I break only those barriers that have been set up by men."

"The priests at the Temple in Jerusalem tell us that all the laws—all the barriers—have been set by God."

"They tell you wrongly," Jesus said.

"But don't they honor the laws given by Moses?" Lazarus asked in surprise.

"There was a time they did. But now . . . now, it is different," Jesus said with a sad look. "The priesthood itself has set up many of the laws."

"Such as?" Mary asked, strangely emboldened by this unusual man.

"Such as the law that requires the separation of men and women at table. Such as the law requiring that a woman who bears a girl child should be considered impure for a longer time than the woman who gives birth to a boy. Such as the law whereby a man may not look upon his wife or daughters in a public place. These are not laws of God. These are laws of men. They are impractical. They cause people to be separated in spirit."

"But . . . the old covenant . . ." Lazarus started to protest.

Jesus quickly interrupted him. "I bring to you a new covenant that deals with the truth and with the spirit of God's Law."

They sat in silence, wondering at this new teaching, trying to absorb the fullness of its meaning, in awe of this guest who was so different from any other who had ever shared their table.

After a long moment Lazarus motioned for Zoë to have the food served. She obeyed quickly as if relieved at activity. And when the food was placed on the table, she retired from the room, taking the other servant with her.

Lazarus turned to Jesus. "Will you bless this meal, Rabboni?"

He agreed, and prayed, "Our Father, Great and Merciful God, we praise your holy name and give you all thanks for providing for our every need." With the prayer concluded, he picked up a small loaf of bread, broke it, and passed the pieces to each of them. "May the nourishment of our new friendship be to our spirits what the nourishment of this bread is to our bodies."

For the most part, the meal was eaten in silence. Jesus and Lazarus both ate heartily. Martha and Mary, however, barely nibbled at the bread Jesus had passed to them and ignored all the other dishes. Any hunger they may have felt was subdued by the strangeness of the situation. And when at last the meal was completed, it was with relief that Martha got to her feet and announced she would bring Simon in to meet Jesus.

He stopped her. "I will go to him, Martha."

"Very well."

Jesus stood up to follow her.

Mary got up to go with them, but Lazarus said, "Perhaps we should wait."

She looked at him in surprise.

"For Simon's sake. He won't want an audience."

"Not even us?"

"Not even us."

Reluctantly Mary sat down again as Martha and Jesus disappeared through the doorway.

They crossed the garden, and when they reached the huge almond tree, Martha paused. "Please, let me tell him you are waiting to meet him."

Jesus gave a nod of understanding.

Martha went toward the reed enclosure just beyond

the almond tree. "Simon, my husband. Jesus is here to see you."

Simon did not respond.

"Will you come out to meet him?"

Still there was no response.

"Please, my husband."

"He cannot help me. Why do you pester me?"

Angry disappointment welled up and flushed hot into Martha's face.

A soft breath of almond-scented air stirred against the lengthening shadows of the day.

"How do you know he cannot help you?"

"No one can help me."

"Let him be the judge of that!"

"Go away!"

"You are an ingrate, Simon of Bethany!"

"Go away, I say. And take the preacher with you!"

Watching from the doorway of the house, Mary began to cry. Lazarus swore under his breath.

Upset and embarrassed, Martha turned away from the reed shelter and hid her face in her hands.

Jesus went to her and put a strengthening hand on her shoulder. "Simon will come to me one day. In his own time, he will come. Until then we must be patient. And you must believe that all will be well. You must believe that."

4

IN the weeks following Jesus' first visit to their house, they thought and spoke of him often.

The question of his identity was constantly in their minds. Mary was certain that he was the Son of God, the messiah, because of what she had seen and heard at the river. Martha was skeptical, caught up as she was with worry over Simon and jealousy over Mary's vision. Lazarus was undecided, and Simon was disbelieving.

But whether or not he was the messiah, they liked him and wanted him for a friend. Already they felt close to him, as close as if they had been friends for many years.

"My sisters and I have never made a friendship so quickly with anyone," Lazarus confided to Bulla as they worked together polishing the crown they had crafted for the Lady Herodias. "I feel as if he has always known us. I feel he would do anything for us. Anything."

"And for Simon?" Bulla asked.

Lazarus shook his head in frustration. "Simon is very stubborn."

"But what is so strange," Lazarus went on, "is that Simon's condition seems to have gotten no worse."

"What do you mean?"

"I know this sounds impossible, but . . ." Lazarus hesitated, groping for the right words. "But it is as if the deterioration of the disease has been slowed."

"You mean Simon is healing?"

"He's no worse."

"You think that Jesus is responsible?"

Lazarus shrugged.

"What does Martha think about this?"

"She is still angry about Simon's refusal to meet Jesus. And . . ."

"And?"

"And she thinks that Simon is delaying his healing by his unbelief."

"Unbelief?"

"Yes. Martha is convinced that Simon's own unbelief is a barrier to Jesus' healing powers."

"Maybe Jesus does not really have such powers," Bulla suggested.

"Oh, I am sure he has," Lazarus said. "John the Baptizer told us he did. That's why we searched everywhere for him. And if Jesus is who my sister Mary says he is, it could well be so."

"Who does Mary say he is?"

"The Son of God."

Bulla put down the small engraving tool and studied Lazarus's face for a long moment. They had worked together for many years. He knew him to be a level-headed man, not prone to flights of fancy about people. But he also knew him as a sensitive man who, beyond his compassion for Simon, was ashamed of and frightened by the kind of illness that beset his brother-in-law. Was his concern for Simon now causing him to think irrationally?

The bell at the entrance to the shop jangled abruptly.

Both men glanced up as a short, squat man, finely dressed in a tunic bearing the emblem of the royal court of Herod Antipas, came through the shop entrance.

"Cover this," Lazarus ordered, pointing to the crown. He stood up and quickly went forward to intercept and greet the officer.

"Are you Lazarus, the silversmith?"

"I am," Lazarus replied with a short bow, recognizing the costly ring on the man's right hand as a design created by his own workmen. The signet of office suspended about the man's neck on a golden chain had been created by them, too. Both had been ordered by Herod Antipas. "How can I be of service, sir?"

"I am Chuza, minister of households for his eminence Herod Antipas."

Lazarus knew the name. Many people considered Chuza the third most powerful man in Judea, after Pontius Pilate and Herod Antipas. He was known to outrank Manaen, Herod's half-brother, in terms of influence at court. And it was claimed that sometimes his advice was heeded by the Romans when even Herod's was not. "You honor my shop with your presence, sir." Lazarus bowed again.

"My lord Herod has sent me to you." He glanced around the shop, nodded to Bulla, then asked, "May I speak with you in confidence?"

"Of course. Bulla is the only workman in the shop at the moment, and I trust him completely."

Chuza stepped closer. "Does he, too, know of the item you are creating for the Lady Herodias?"

Lazarus nodded. "Bulla himself measured the lady's head for the cr—"

Chuza held up a warning hand and glanced over his shoulder toward the shop's open entrance. The street was crowded. Four or five Pharisees were huddled together in agitated conversation just beyond the entrance to the shop. Chuza eyed them carefully; then apparently satisfied that none of them could overhear him, he turned again to Lazarus. "My lord Herod wishes to know when the item will be ready for delivery."

"It is ready. Bulla and I were just giving it a final polish."

A brief smile flickered on Chuza's face. "You, indeed, are prompt. My lord Herod told me that this was the day you had promised the creation. I would like to see it."

Lazarus turned and led the way to the workbench and introduced Bulla to Chuza.

Bulla acknowledged the introduction and uncovered the secret work.

Chuza gasped in approval at the beauty of it. The circlet of the crown was a delicate, lacelike openwork of gold and silver. At intervals along the intertwining threads were designs of acanthus leaves and ivy. Inset among these designs were choice emeralds, rubies, and sapphires. A taller front piece featured a trellis effect implanted with a large and singularly beautiful emerald.

"Magnificent!" Chuza exclaimed.

Bulla beamed with pride at the compliment and began to detail the work involved. "The front piece is strong to hold the great emerald but yet is in balance with the circlet so that the piece will rest evenly on the head of the Lady Herodias."

"It is a wonderful piece of work," Chuza said. "I wish I could afford such a thing for my own wife."

Lazarus glanced at him in surprise.

"Oh, not a crown," Chuza laughed. "By the gods, not a crown at all. But a wonderful piece of jewelry. A bracelet, or bangles for the ears, or a necklace."

"We have some of each of those items," Lazarus said, quickly turning toward a cupboard where the better pieces were hidden.

But Chuza stopped him with a gesture and another laugh. "Not this time, silversmith. Perhaps later, after the court has returned to Jerusalem. Perhaps then I'll come to make a purchase for my wife."

"Very well, sir."

Bulla spoke up. "We have only a touch more polishing to be done on the piece for the Lady Herodias. Then we must carefully wrap it."

"It will not take long," Lazarus reassured him. "In the meantime, come and take refreshment with me." He moved toward the front of the shop again, where two reed and leather stools were situated near a small cabinet. "I keep a supply of wine here in the shop. For our customers. You would honor me by having some."

"Your hospitality is welcomed." Chuza sat down and glanced around the shop. "You've done work for Herod Antipas for many years, haven't you?"

Lazarus nodded.

"I saw you, and your workman, at the palace in Jericho. But it's strange I've never seen you here in this shop before."

"It's usually my partner, Simon of Bethany, who takes care of greeting our customers and doing the selling.

My work is more on the design and crafting side of the business."

"Ah, yes, Simon of Bethany. Big, gruff man. Now, I recall. But he wasn't with you in Jericho, was he?"

Lazarus handed a cup of wine to Chuza before giving a careful answer to the question. "No, Simon has not been well in recent weeks. He was not with me in Jericho."

"I'm sorry to hear of that. It's nothing serious, I hope."

"I shall pass your greeting to Simon," Lazarus said, and, hoping to avoid further talk of Simon's illness, he quickly changed the subject. "Is the tetrarch still in Jericho?"

Chuza drained his wine cup. "The tetrarch is now at the Fortress Machaerus. He and the royal court have been there for several days. And the plan is that we'll remain there for several weeks."

Lazarus refilled the wine cup for his guest. "It would seem that Jerusalem would be much cooler than Machaerus this time of year."

"Indeed, it would be! But surely the tetrarch told you of his plan to give the crown to the Lady Herodias at Machaerus."

"Of course," Lazarus shook his head apologetically. "I should have remembered that."

"I think it's a great risk to give such a gift to her," Chuza said in abrupt candor. "If the Romans learn of this, there will be more trouble. Already there is outrage and a public outcry over the imprisonment of that wilderness preacher."

"You mean the Baptizer?"

Chuza nodded.

"Is he now imprisoned?"

Chuza leaned toward him. "He is."

"Why should Herod want to imprison him? It only makes him more important, doesn't it?"

"That is exactly how I counseled the tetrarch," Chuza said, looking at Lazarus with new respect. "But the tetrarch will do anything to appease his lady. So he now has the preacher imprisoned at Machaerus." Chuza stared moodily at his wine cup for a moment then leaned and looked out toward the street where the Pharisees had been gathered.

"Is something wrong, sir?" Lazarus asked.

"I feel overly cautious today, silversmith. The Pharisees and other members of the Sanhedrin are delighted that the Baptizer is in prison. They're now pressing a search for a man that was baptized by the preacher who is proclaimed to be the Son of God."

A pang of fear shot through Lazarus.

"Have you heard any talk of such a person?"

Lazarus shook his head.

"We don't need a religious uprising in Judea," Chuza went on, holding out his cup for Lazarus to pour more wine. "But we well could have it. And then there is this . . . this . . . crown thing!"

Bulla came to them carrying the crown carefully wrapped in soft cloths and handed it to Chuza.

Chuza drained his cup again, set it down, and took the bundle from Bulla. For a brief moment he inspected it then slipped it inside his tunic. "Next to my heart is the best place to carry this," he said with a humorless chuckle. "I bid you and your workman farewell, silversmith."

Lazarus and Bulla bowed almost in unison as Chuza went out of the shop and disappeared in the crowded street.

At the end of the day, when Lazarus arrived back at

the house in Bethany, he found Martha and Timora, a neighbor, in intense conversation.

"They have arrested John the Baptizer," Martha said. "And they are now searching for Jesus."

"I know," said Lazarus with a weary shake of his head. "One of Herod's men was in the shop today and told us."

"I am glad that Jesus is safely back in Galilee," Martha said.

Lazarus looked at her in wonderment. For so strongly opinionated a person, she was amazingly naive. "The power of the Sanhedrin reaches into Galilee, too, my sister."

"They will not find him," she said airily, as if privy to all of Jesus' plans.

"I hope you're right, Martha," said Timora.

"So do I!" Lazarus agreed.

Martha seemed to ignore their skepticism, thanked Timora for bringing her the news about the Baptizer, and as the neighbor left, walked back into the garden.

Lazarus followed her, unwilling to argue but carrying a heavier and heavier weight of worry about their new friend Jesus.

As they reached the almond tree, Martha paused. "There is other news that has come to us today, too. And it is much happier news."

"Happier? Then I shall be glad to hear it."

"The son of Zeppha of Cana is to be married. We are invited to come to the wedding. I want to go. Can we do it? Will your work allow it?"

Lazarus nodded. "My work will allow it. The special item for the tetrarch is finished. Bulla and the others can handle the shop while I'm away, I suppose. Does Mary want to go, too?"

"She does."

"What about Simon?"

"Zoë will look after him."

Lazarus pulled a twig from the almond tree. "Then there is nothing to stop us, is there?"

"It will be good to see happiness all around us again," Martha said, a faraway look in her eyes.

Lazarus suddenly understood how deeply she mourned Simon's condition. He leaned toward her and kissed her gently on the forehead. "I'll go and tell Simon that we are going to the wedding in Cana. When should we leave?"

"No later than the day after tomorrow."

5

CANA, in Galilee, was a six-day journey from
Bethany, in Judea, for Martha, Mary, Lazarus, and two
of their servants. They chose to travel northward through
Perea along the eastern shore of the River Jordan rather
than by the more direct route through the land of
Samaria. Samaritans were not friendly to Jews. Bad feelings had existed between the two peoples for many generations. It was a particularly unsafe route to travel if valu-
ables were being carried, such as the wedding gifts
Lazarus had brought along.

And so the family and two servants made their way up
the winding, tortuous trail on Jordan's eastern shore until
they could safely cross back to the west and into Galilee,
just below the southern end of the Sea of Galilee. Even
at this point, however, they were still some distance from
Cana. It was situated in northern Galilee, a half day's
journey beyond Nazareth and a day's journey northwest
of Tiberias, the sparkling new capital city built on the
shore of the Sea of Galilee by Herod Antipas in honor of
the Romans' emperor.

On the outskirts of Tiberias, in a village called

Amaathus, they broke their journey for a day and finally arrived in Cana late on the day before the wedding ceremony was to occur.

A number of other guests from long distances were already there with tents set up close to Zeppha's house. The only remaining space was under a giant acacia at the edge of Zeppha's property. Martha complained about how far they were from Zeppha's house.

"This is a good location," Lazarus pointed out to her. "Think how noisy it is near the house."

"I like it, too," Mary agreed. "It's cool in the shade of this wonderful old tree. And if the crowd gets too large, or too noisy, we can retreat!"

"Oh, very well!" Martha conceded. "Besides, we have no other choice, do we?"

"It's not likely," Lazarus grinned, heading off for the house to let Zeppha know they had arrived.

Martha turned to the servants and instructed them to set up the tents, while she and Mary began to prepare the evening meal. It was a simple one of bread, cheese, and fruit, and required no cooking fire. But as the sun retired beyond Galilee's lovely green hills, a coolness filtered through the air that was unfamiliar and unexpected. Mary shivered. Martha instructed the servant Joachim to make a fire against the oncoming chill. He did so, and shortly thereafter Lazarus returned accompanied by a stranger.

"My sisters," he said, "This is Levi of Capernaum. He is a cousin to Zeppha's wife. We can call him Zeppha's Steward of the Wedding Gifts."

Levi smiled at the name Lazarus gave him and bowed in acknowledgment of the introduction to Martha and Mary.

"He has come to help me carry the gifts we've brought to Zeppha's house," Lazarus said.

"You're welcome to share our meal, sir," Martha said, motioning for him to be seated.

"That is kind of you. But I don't wish to intrude."

"It will be no intrusion," Lazarus said. "You will honor us by sharing a meal."

Levi hesitated, looking at Mary with interest, apparently wanting her approval of the invitation, too.

Mary glanced at him but with quick shyness lowered her eyes and remained silent.

"Pay no attention to my younger sister," Lazarus laughed. "She welcomes you, in spite of her silence."

Mary blushed so red that it was noticeable against the firelight. She straightened uncomfortably and busied herself with unwrapping another of the cheeses Martha had set out on the soft rug that was serving as a table for the meal.

Levi seated himself beside her.

She avoided looking at him.

Martha, however, exhibited no such lack of interest. She gazed at him directly in an inspective manner. He was a dark man with a fringe of close-cropped beard. He wore a turban and robes of homespun, and about his neck on a leather thong was a signet with a design she had never seen. His eyes were dark but reflected a certain good humor; and he had an air of importance about him, a demeanor of authority.

"Levi is a tax collector, Martha," Lazarus said, as if reading her mind. He sat down beside their guest and offered him one of the loaves of coarse brown bread.

Levi took it, broke off a chunk, and handed the loaf back to Lazarus. "It is a thankless job, the business of collecting taxes."

"I can imagine."

"I sometimes think I was not cut out for it."

"What else would you like to do?" Lazarus asked.

Levi gave a rueful smile, shook his head, and bit into the bread.

"Mary, pass one of those cheeses to our guest," Martha instructed.

Mary did so without looking up.

Levi tried to thank her with a smile.

She took no notice.

Levi broke off a piece of the cheese and handed it to Lazarus. "Zeppha thinks I should be a rabbi," he said unexpectedly.

Mary looked at him now and, like Martha had before, inspected him directly.

"Why should Zeppha think that?" Lazarus asked.

"He says I am too open-hearted, and too openhanded to be a good tax collector. He says that someday the Romans will come to think that, too. And then I shall have to give this signet to my successor." He fingered the signet on the leather thong. "But I keep telling him I would be a poor choice for a rabbi. That just because I read and write and can handle sums does not qualify me as a wise man. And that's what a rabbi should be. A wise man. Don't you think so?"

Lazarus and Martha exchanged glances of surprise at his unexpected candor. They barely knew him.

"He should talk with Jesus," Mary said quietly. "Jesus can help him to know what to do."

All three of them looked at her in abrupt surprise, Levi more puzzled than the other two. "Who is Jesus?"

"A teacher of great wisdom," Lazarus said.

"A friend of ours," Martha added. "He comes from Nazareth. And my brother is right, Jesus is a man of wisdom. He is also . . ." She stopped suddenly, realizing that she would be unwise to say what was in her mind about Jesus' being a breaker of barriers. After all, the tax collector's apparent candor could be misleading.

"He is also what?" Levi wanted to know, glancing from Martha to Lazarus to Mary.

"You should talk to him," Mary repeated. "He can help to direct your life."

"Where can I find this Jesus?"

"He is from Nazareth, as my sister told you."

"I never have been to Nazareth, nor have I ever had a reason to go there."

Mary shrugged. "Perhaps then he will come to you, as he came to us."

The puzzled look again crossed Levi's face.

Lazarus explained to him how he had met Jesus on the Jericho road, how their friendship began, how Jesus had accepted their invitation to stay with them for a day or two, how quickly they all felt close to him and had offered their home to him whenever he wanted to come.

Caught up in the memory of Jesus' visit, Martha was again prompted to tell Levi about what a breaker of barriers Jesus was but again thought better of it. She didn't know Levi well enough yet to share such a startling truth with him.

Mary withdrew into silence, meditative, lost in her memories of the vision she had seen at the river when Jesus was baptized.

Levi got up. "Your hospitality has been a solace to my soul. I must return now to the house of my cousin's husband." He bowed to Martha and Mary.

Lazarus got up, too. "Let me fetch the wedding gifts."

The next morning dawned bright and clear for the

wedding of Zeppha's son and his bride. More family members and friends from nearby villages came to witness the ceremony. There were flowers and music, dancing and laughter, food and wine. Joyfulness was everywhere. The wedding feast had been set up under thatch shades in a garden near the house. Food of every variety ladened the tables. Great jars of new wine were lined up in the coolest part of the shade. Zeppha's servants dipped small serving pitchers into the great jars, filling them with the fragrant liquid, and then moved ceaselessly back and forth among the guests serving it.

"It reminds me of your wedding to Simon," Mary whispered to Martha as she watched all the festivity.

Tears suddenly brimmed in Martha's eyes.

"Oh, I'm sorry to make you cry," Mary said quickly, slipping her arm around Martha's waist. "It is all so beautiful. And your wedding was beautiful, too."

Martha wiped at the tears with a corner of her head scarf and tried to smile.

"Please don't cry," Mary pleaded. "I can't stand it when you cry."

"I know," Martha patted Mary's hand reassuringly. "It's just that . . . Simon and I were so very happy to find each other all those years ago. And now . . ."

"It's the illness. The disease makes him so much more gruff than ever," said Mary.

"And it makes me such a . . . such a blunt woman."

"Jesus will help him."

Martha wiped away her tears. "If Simon will only let him."

"Someday Simon will."

"And if Jesus ever comes to visit us again," Martha complained. "It has been three months or more."

"What has been three months or more?" Lazarus was coming toward them, and when he noticed that Martha had been crying, he asked quickly, "What has happened? Why are you crying?"

Mary explained.

"And what has the three months or more got to do with it?"

"I just commented that it has been that long since we saw Jesus." She gave an apologetic smile. "Maybe I was even complaining about it."

"Well, complain no more. Jesus is here!"

They both looked at him in astonishment.

He nodded his head with an enthusiastic smile. "Come! Come and greet him."

They followed as Lazarus led them through the throng of guests to a spot under the shade of a great mustard bush, where Jesus stood talking with four men. When Lazarus hailed him, Jesus turned, recognized the three of them, smiled, and opened his arms in welcome.

Martha and Mary went down on their knees in a deep curtsy of respect.

He came to them, stretched forth his hands, and lifted them to their feet. "Martha. Mary. How good it is to see you." He turned to Lazarus. "My friend, you look well."

"As do you, Jesus," Lazarus responded.

Jesus motioned for the four men to come and join them. "I want you and your sisters to know my men. This is Peter."

The largest of the four stepped forward, nodded, and gave a casual salute to Lazarus.

"This is Andrew, brother to Peter."

The family resemblance was strong, but he was

smaller than his brother, and he only nodded acknowledgment of the introduction.

"This is James, son of Zebedee, the fisherman of Bethsaida and Capernaum."

The man was wiry and tense looking. He gave a slight nod without taking his eyes off Lazarus and the women.

"And this is John, brother to James."

Though he was obviously the youngest of the four, he was almost as tall as Peter. His hair was a dark auburn color. He bowed. The motion made flecks of reddish gold appear in his hair. He straightened and gave them a look of direct and open friendliness with just a hint of an impish grin.

"These are my friends who live in Bethany of Judea," Jesus said. "They are the hospitable people I have told you about. They have offered their home to me as openly as your father, James and John, has opened his. And they welcome me as cordially as you and your family welcome me, Peter."

"We thank you for your hospitality to our master," Peter said, his voice deep and rumbling as thunder in summer. "He is teaching us that such hospitality will not be his, nor ours, everywhere."

Lazarus smiled. "Your men are also welcome at our house, Jesus. I want you to know that."

Jesus turned to Martha. "Do you agree with your brother? Will you want your house filled from time to time with an itinerant preacher and his men?"

Surprise came onto the men's faces. Custom provided no such confirming power to a woman. It was a man's province to say who should be welcomed in his home.

Seeing the looks, Mary reddened and took a step back. Lazarus laughed. And Martha smiled.

"When you get to know this family better," Jesus said, "you will understand why I ask such a question."

"It is because my sister owns the house, for one thing," Lazarus said.

"And it is because I am a blunt and bossy woman! As Jesus already knows," Martha added in all good humor.

Fresh surprise appeared on the men's faces.

Jesus chuckled. "Such candor from a woman is a new experience. But these men will learn, Martha. They will learn!"

Levi approached.

Lazarus hailed him. "This is the teacher we told you about, Levi. This is Jesus of Nazareth. And these are his men."

Levi bowed. "I bid you welcome to the house of my cousin's husband."

Jesus searched him with a penetrating gaze, particularly seeming to notice the signet of office about his neck. "In what place do you collect the taxes for Caesar?"

"Capernaum."

"Your face is not familiar to us," James challenged.

"And James certainly would remember the face of a tax collector!" John added with a grin.

Levi laughed a bit nervously. "I admit that it is not the most popular job a man can have. On the other hand, hunger is not popular with me, either." When the laughter died down, he turned again to Jesus. "You do the house of my cousin's husband great honor by your presence. I am pleased to learn that he is a friend of yours. In fact, I may want to intrude on that friendship."

"It is my mother who has the friendship of this house," Jesus told him.

"Oh, I see."

"I have come here with her, and her family," Jesus finished.

The answer bewildered Levi, and he wondered why Jesus had spoken in such a way. But no one else seemed curious about it, as if they hadn't heard, and that, too, seemed odd.

"But how is it you wish to intrude on the friendship?" Jesus asked, again pinning him with a penetrating gaze.

"Oh . . . uh . . . it is nothing."

"What Levi wants to say, Jesus," Lazarus put in, "is that he has need of your counsel."

"Perhaps at some more convenient time," Levi demurred.

"My men and I are on our way to Capernaum to meet two others of our group, Nathanael and Philip. Come with us, if you like."

Levi nodded, but before he could do more in the way of accepting Jesus' invitation, a woman and two stalwart young men approached.

John leaned close to Jesus and said, "Your mother and two of your brothers are coming."

Jesus turned to greet them and introduced them to Levi and the family from Bethany.

Jesus' mother acknowledged the introductions with a gracious bow. She was a small woman. Her face held a look of unusual radiance, and she seemed quite young to have sons as old as Jesus and the two young men who were with her. "My son, our host finds himself embarrassed."

"In what way?"

"There is no more wine."

A strange look came over Jesus' face. He clasped his mother by the arm and gently led her away from the rest. "You put temptation before me, my mother. Why?"

"You can help our host out of this embarrassment," Martha heard her say. "I know you can help, if you but will."

They walked on toward the garden where the wine jars were located. Peter and John, Martha and Lazarus, and Jesus' two brothers followed. When Jesus and his mother reached the edge of the thatch shade, Jesus hesitated, then let go of his mother's arm.

She walked on, going to Zeppha's servants and saying to them, "Whatever my son tells you to do, do it." Then she left the garden shade, her two other sons following.

Martha and Lazarus looked at each other in wonderment and turned to Peter and John for an explanation.

John shrugged.

And Peter ignored them. His eyes were on Jesus, who now slowly walked toward six stone waterpots resting nearby.

Jesus inspected the waterpots with deliberate care.

In fact, he deliberated over them for such a long time that Martha thought he seemed to be in a trance.

Yet when he turned to the servants standing nearby, his eyes were bright and his face naturally expressive. "Fill these pots with water to the brim," he instructed in a soft voice.

The servants did as he said.

He inspected the waterpots once more and said to one of the servants, "Draw some out and take it to the governor of the feast." He then turned and motioned for his men to follow. They all went in the direction his mother had taken. Levi went with them.

Mary came to Martha and Lazarus. "What was he doing?"

"Sh-h-h," Martha warned. But as the servant drew the liquid from the waterpots into serving pitchers, she herself gasped aloud in spite of the warning given to Mary. The water now being poured had the color of a fine, dry white wine. Enchanted at the very idea, she followed the servant as he carried the pitcher into the house and served the governor, Zeppha, and Zeppha's son, the bridegroom.

The governor sipped at the liquid, smiled, and turning to Zeppha, proclaimed, "Everyone serves good wine first and the worst wine when the guests have already drunk their fill. But you have kept the best wine until last!"

"It is a miracle," Martha murmured in astonishment. "It is a miracle!"

"His powers are greater than other men's, by far. By far." Lazarus said, coming up beside her, disbelief in his voice.

"How can this be?" Martha whispered.

"It is a revelation of his glory," Mary said with quiet assurance. "A true revelation of his glory. I told you before, he is the Son of God!"

"I must talk to him about Simon," Martha said, turning away from the doorway of Zeppha's house. "I must ask him to come back to Bethany and heal Simon. At once. If he can turn water into wine, he can heal Simon whether or not Simon believes it!"

"Jesus is no longer here," Lazarus said, pointing to the road that led off eastward toward Capernaum. "He has left before all the guests disturb the wedding feast with questions about the wine."

Martha turned just in time to see Jesus, his men, his mother and brothers, and Levi disappear over a hill. She started after them.

Lazarus stopped her. "This is not the proper way for us, my sister."

"I've never seen you so impulsive," Mary chided. "It's not like you."

"And the leprosy is not like Simon!" She threw the words at them out of frustration and fear.

"It is still important that Simon believes this can be done for him," Lazarus reminded her. "The water would never have been turned into wine if Jesus' mother had not believed he could do it! Simon will not be healed until Simon believes it can happen."

Martha pulled away from Lazarus and stared moodily into the distance before accepting the wisdom of her brother's words. "Then let us leave for home. At once. We must tell Simon of the miracle we have seen."

Lazarus shook his head. "We can't leave now. It would offend the household of Zeppha. You know the custom. We must stay at least until tomorrow."

"At least until tomorrow," Mary echoed.

Martha turned abruptly and walked away.

Mary caught up with her. "Rudeness does not become you, my sister. Do you think it will help for you to be so demanding?"

6

Six months had passed since the family witnessed Jesus' miracle of turning water into wine. In the same six months they had continued to witness another miracle, one measured by the fact that Simon's disease appeared to have grown no worse. It seemed to be no better, but certainly no worse.

Since Jesus had been a guest in the house, Simon's disease seemed totally unchanged, suspended, inert, nonmalevolent. The lack of change affected the mood of the entire household. Simon's gruffness seemed to soften. Martha seemed more at ease. She was less demanding, less aggressive about having her own way. Mary no longer felt so troubled about the welfare of her sister and brother-in-law. And Lazarus began to enjoy his work more than at any time since Simon got sick.

But there were other changes taking place in other parts of Judea that would also affect the household, and in far less positive ways.

Within a few weeks of their return from Cana, Timora and another neighbor brought the news that John the

Baptizer had been beheaded in the prison of the Fortress Machaerus. Herodias had insisted on it. Herod Antipas had ordered it done.

Quickly following this news came word that Jesus was preaching, and teaching, and healing almost daily in Galilee. Those who heard him told others, and the crowds grew until hundreds, sometimes thousands, of people gathered to hear him. Many followed him everywhere. The impact of his message was strong. Lives were changed. Many people were healed of diverse diseases. But when word of all these miracles—all this spiritual power—came to the Sanhedrin, the priesthood, and the court of Herod Antipas, territorial instincts were agitated. Fear reigned.

"He is preaching outside the synagogues. On hillsides!" a Sadducee complained to Caiaphas, the high priest.

"He and his men, all twelve of them, travel on the Sabbath! They even helped a man pull an ox out of a ditch on the Sabbath. They picked ears of corn and ate them. On the Sabbath!"

"Good Jews don't work on the Sabbath! Good Jews don't travel on the Sabbath. It is forbidden by the Law."

"He treats women almost as equals," said another Pharisee, the phylactery jangling in agitation on his forehead.

"The Law says a man must not even look upon a woman in public!"

When the news was brought to Herod Antipas that Jesus healed the son of a nobleman without even seeing or being with the boy, he bellowed in disbelief, "What kind of fool do you take me for?"

Manaen, his half-brother, insisted, "My lackey was there. He saw it! The nobleman merely said to Jesus, 'My son is ill. I know you can heal him.' And Jesus replied, 'Your son is healed. Your faith has made it so!' And when my lackey followed the nobleman on his way to his home, he saw the servants of the nobleman running to him to announce that the son was well!"

"I still don't believe it!"

"What we really should worry about," Chuza said carefully, "is the message this man Jesus is preaching."

"What is the message?"

"That a new kingdom is at hand, sire!"

A deep frown crossed Herod's face. He pushed up off the chair and paced the length of the royal chambers. "A new kingdom, indeed. There is enough religious and political unrest in the land without such a threat as that!" He came back to Chuza. "We don't need some ragged preacher from Galilee fomenting riots with such lies."

"You're quite right, your Excellency," Chuza agreed. "But the—"

Manaen interrupted. "But the truth of the matter is, my dear brother, that you are responsible for most of that unrest."

"I? I am responsible for fomenting unrest?"

"Yes, you are! You gave in to Herodias!"

The swarthy face darkened. "Don't mention that!"

"You had John the Baptizer beheaded," Manaen charged.

"I don't want to hear any more about it!" Herod shouted, turning on his half-brother.

"Many of your subjects are outraged! They are ready to incite a riot. You are responsible."

"Quiet, I say!"

Manaen shrugged. "It's still true! It's a political fact we must deal with!"

A servant slipped into the royal chambers and whispered in Chuza's ear.

"I beg your indulgence, your Excellency," Chuza said, welcoming a chance to break up the argument. "A delegation from the Sanhedrin has arrived. They await an audience with your Eminence."

Herod swiveled about. "What do they want?"

"I don't know, your Excellency."

"I'll talk to them for you," Manaen said.

"You'll do no such thing!"

Chuza stepped between them. "If you please, your Excellency, let me go and inquire of their need. Then you will know whether or not their need is worth your time."

The darkness in Herod's face lightened a bit. He nodded his approval, and Chuza quickly departed to greet the delegation.

Within moments he was back.

"Well?" Herod demanded.

"They want to talk about the Galilean preacher."

Herod strode in agitation around the royal chambers.

"See them," Manaen urged. "Soothe them, if you can. Don't let this turn into another beheading like with John the Baptizer!"

"By the eyes of all the gods, Manaen—"

"Your brother may be right, sire," Chuza ventured, walking to the long worktable at one side of the room and fingering the large parchment that had come from the Sanhedrin several days before, and which he knew

Herod had not read. "It might save a lot of dry reading, sire."

Herod turned and glared at him. "Who is in the delegation?"

"Joseph of Arimathea, the merchant, Nicodemus the banker, and the high priest, Joseph Caiaphas."

"Only three?"

"Only those three, sire."

"No Pharisees to threaten me with their self-righteous hypocrisy and their clattering phylacteries?"

Chuza shook his head.

"Very well. Bring them in."

Chuza nodded and went to fetch the delegation.

Herod went to the Roman-style chair he used as a royal throne, sat down, and clasped its arms in a gesture of permanent possession.

Manaen walked to the far side of the chambers and leaned against the wall to wait and watch.

Chuza returned, leading the delegation to the prescribed distance allowed for those seeking audience. Then he backed away to stand near Manaen.

The delegation bowed. It was Joseph of Arimathea, known to be respected by Herod, who spoke first. "Your Eminence, there is a controversy among us. Thus we have come seeking your counsel."

"On what subject?"

"The preacher Jesus."

"On that subject perhaps it should be I who seeks your counsel." He cast a cynical look at Manaen.

"Sire?" Nicodemus and Caiaphas spoke at the same time, their eyes wide in astonishment. Herod never sought advice from the Sanhedrin, no matter the subject.

"I have heard the reports about this man Jesus," Herod said, breaking into their astonishment.

"And you are not fearful?" Caiaphas almost gasped the question.

"Fearful? Why should I be fearful?"

Herod said it in a tone of such complete indifference that Manaen and Chuza exchanged looks of surprise.

"After all, this is a religious matter, not a government matter. Why should I be fearful?"

"But the man Jesus preaches about a new kingdom."

"He says it is at hand," Nicodemus added. "It is a threat to you, Herod, as much as to the Sanhedrin and the priesthood—and the economy!"

"A threat?" Herod feigned disbelief. "How can he be a threat? Has he an army?"

They shook their heads.

"Does he have influence with people of importance?"

Again they shook their heads.

"Then how can you think this Jesus is a threat to me, or to the Sanhedrin and the priesthood?"

"But people are flocking to him by the thousands," Caiaphas said. "He is influencing them mightily. We have spies in Galilee who mingle among the people, who listen to what they are saying. They are quite loyal to Jesus. And all manner of strange and wonderful happenings occur."

Herod turned to Joseph. "And what of your trade, merchant. How is Jesus' influence on the people affecting your business?"

Joseph gave an enigmatic smile. "In all truth, your Eminence, I cannot see that his preaching has had an effect on my business, one way or the other."

"Then why do you come here with Nicodemus and Caiaphas?"

"Because I, too, have a concern about all of this. I have a curiosity about it. And therein lies the controversy between the three of us." He pointed to Caiaphas and Nicodemus.

"You have a curiosity? In what way?"

"In so far as the fulfillment of prophecy is concerned."

"The fulfillment of prophecy?"

"Yes, sire. In the Torah, prophecy holds that one day a man will be born who holds the wisdom of the ages in his mind and the powers of the one true God in his hands. For those who are Jews and believe in Jewish ways, this man will be protector, provider, savior. The Jews' messiah. The more I hear about the man Jesus, the more my curiosity causes me to wonder if—"

A sudden burst of laughter erupted from Herod. He rose from his chair and paced. "You? You, merchant? You think this preacher in Galilee is your messiah?"

Joseph watched impassively, but resentment sparked in his eyes. He stood quite still while Herod continued to laugh and pace about.

Caiaphas and Nicodemus stood still. Though they did not agree with Joseph, he was too important a man to make sport of, such as Herod seemed to be doing.

Manaen came forward and spoke softly to Herod. "The Arimathean is a wise man, my brother. And he is important to us. Too much laughter may be ill timed. Offer him and the others some wine. Soothe him. Soothe them all. Hear what else they may have to say."

Herod nodded and sat back down.

Manaen signaled for Chuza to have servants bring wine.

"A thousand apologies, my friend," Herod said. "My laughter was not meant for you as much as it was meant for the improbabilities of the very idea." He leaned forward, resting an elbow on one knee. "This man Jesus has no money. I am told that he is a carpenter by trade. He has no army. He has no weapons. And yet you are seriously thinking he will bring in a new kingdom and change the world?"

"I seriously think that is a possibility," Joseph said quietly.

Herod sat back and stared at him.

Two servants came bearing wine, cups, and three chairs for the visitors. Herod motioned for them to be seated.

As they sipped at their wine, Herod said to Nicodemus and Caiaphas, "Since you two don't agree with the merchant, what do you think of Jesus?"

"He preaches heresy," Caiaphas said quickly. "He is a rabble-rouser. He defies our customs and our laws. He must be stopped. And he must be stopped now!"

"And you, Nicodemus? Do you share the feeling Caiaphas has expressed?"

"I do, my lord. Jesus is bad for the economy. He is bad for business."

"And how do you propose he be stopped?" Herod asked, motioning for a servant to come and refill his wine cup.

"There are laws against murder, sire. Even the murder of preachers who preach truths that we don't agree with!" Joseph spoke the words in such a gentle tone that it took a moment for Herod to realize he was referring to the beheading of John the Baptizer.

But the inference was immediately clear to all the others in the royal chambers. Caiaphas and Nicodemus studied their wine cups uneasily. Chuza and Manaen looked at each other and tensed, alert for Herod's anger. Joseph, however, gazed at Herod and waited, patient and fearless.

Herod met Joseph's gaze with eyes blazing. His hand trembled a bit as he held out the wine cup to the servant.

"Of course, there are extenuating circumstances," Joseph said, still watching Herod, "that warrant such an evil act as murder. But only within the confines of our laws. And in the case of the man Jesus, it is doubtful he has broken any of our laws."

Caiaphas suddenly found his voice. "Oh, but he has!"

"Then arrest him, high priest!" Herod stood up.

The others rose, too.

"You came seeking my counsel. Arrest this Jesus of Nazareth. If necessary, kill him. That is my counsel." He turned and left the royal chambers.

7

MARTHA and Zoë hurried along the Street of the Sheep's Gate toward the shop, carrying baskets of food for Lazarus, Bulla, and the other workmen. A large order from the Romans for the repair of breastplates had kept the men at work night and day. They even slept in the shop on rough straw mats, taking turns so that the work never halted. Martha brought them food and drink twice each day.

Even though it was still early in the day, her delivery was later than usual, and she was in a hurry. But two men directly ahead, going in the same direction, were dawdling along deep in conversation. "Walk faster, Zoë. We will go around them," she said, impatiently glancing back at her servant.

"It matters not whether I do or don't, mistress. The street is blocked for us both." She nodded at a shepherd with a small flock of sheep coming toward them.

With an impatient sigh, Martha accepted the situation and slowed down. The two men dawdling in front of her were obviously men of importance. They were dressed in the finest of robes. And, she decided, they must be discussing a very important matter, so intent were they on their conversation.

"There will be an aftermath to this morning's meeting with the tetrarch," the short, round man said to his taller companion.

"I agree. Not even Joseph of Arimathea can speak so candidly to Herod without some kind of reprisal."

"What I fear is that such candidness will bring retaliation. Sooner or later Caiaphas will once again seek Herod's help."

"He is not likely to get it," the little round man said in a grim tone. "Caiaphas has already broken his word to Herod. He was supposed to take John the Baptizer off of Herod's hands."

"Oh, yes. Now I remember. Perhaps I was too hard on Herod this morning."

"Not at all. The deed warranted it."

"What do you suppose Caiaphas will finally do about this man Jesus?"

At the mention of Jesus' name, Martha strained forward, trying now to catch every word of the conversation going on in front of her. Zoë moved up next to her, also listening.

"When you were escorting the delegation out of the palace," the taller man went on, "Herod came to me and asked if I thought Jesus was actually John the Baptizer come back to life!"

The short, round man glanced in astonishment at his companion and slowed his pace almost to a standstill.

Martha and Zoë had to stop abruptly to keep from bumping him with the food baskets.

"Can you imagine anything so unrealistic?"

"I cannot." The short, round man shook his head, and resumed walking.

Martha and Zoë moved forward, too, once again, keeping as close as possible to the men without being suspected of eavesdropping.

"Of course, fear makes Herod think unrealistically. We both know that," said the taller man. "And fear makes him do unrealistic things."

"In a way, I understand his fear. Remember, the Romans are constantly at him to keep the civil peace. Herod meant it when he told Caiaphas to arrest Jesus. He wants no trouble with the Romans."

"But can you imagine! Arresting a man who can heal people!" the short man said. "Your own lackey has had his life changed since he witnessed Jesus' healing of the nobleman's son."

The men turned off into another street. Martha stopped, looked at Zoë.

"There must be some way we can use what we just heard to help Jesus," the servant said.

"Yes. And maybe we can help Simon by what we've heard, too."

"Simon?" Martha called out the moment she stepped through the gate and into the garden. "Simon, I have wonderful news for you."

"The Romans have paid Lazarus a fat bonus for all the work the shop has done repairing their breastplates!" he teased from his retreat. "Is that the wonderful news?"

She laughed. "No, my husband, that is not the news. The news I bring is even more wonderful. It is news of Jesus. It is another story of his healing power."

"Oh?"

She launched enthusiastically into the report she'd

heard about his healing the nobleman's son. "Even one of Herod's servants has had his life changed just by having witnessed the healing. It is all wonderful news, isn't it, Simon?"

He was silent for a very long moment.

"Simon? Did you hear me?"

"Yes, I heard you, Martha," he said thoughtfully. The usual cynicism was absent from his tone. In its place was the merest suggestion of acceptance, as if he might already have started to believe in Jesus' healing powers for himself. "Yes, I heard you, Martha," he repeated in an even softer, more reflective tone. "And yes, it is wonderful news."

The joy of new hope sprang into Martha's heart. Tears brimmed in her eyes. "Oh, Simon, does this mean you'll meet with Jesus when next he comes to visit us?"

There was another long moment of silence from the garden retreat. And then Simon said, "It is wonderful news you have brought, my wife. Now I must rest."

The joy of new hope in her heart subsided. She turned away, fighting disappointment, and saw Mary coming toward her from the house, a look of excited questioning on her face.

"What did Simon say? Zoë told me about the healing of the nobleman's son. Is Simon now convinced of Jesus' healing powers?"

With a heavy sigh, Martha shook her head.

The excitement went out of Mary's face.

"We must not stop hoping . . ."

"And praying . . ."

"And praying," she agreed. She linked arms with Mary, accepted with gratefulness the comforting squeeze of her hand.

"Zoë also told me of what you overheard about the threat against Jesus."

Martha gave an absent nod, her mind still on Simon.

"That seems so senseless," Mary's gentle voice held an edge of impatience. "To arrest a man like Jesus! There is so much illness and disease, so much tribulation, so many tragedies. Why would anyone want to arrest a man who can heal?"

She asked the same question of Lazarus three days later when he returned from Jerusalem. The job of repairing breastplates was finished. The Romans were well satisfied with the work and had paid handsomely for it.

"Before they can arrest Jesus," Lazarus answered, "they have to find him. And anyway, if he really is the Son of God, as you think, little sister, they can't arrest him until he lets them!" He turned and went out into the garden to give a report to Simon.

They spoke together for a long time about the business the Romans brought to the shop and about the gossip among the merchants whose shops neighbored their own. At last the conversation turned to Jesus.

"I have changed my mind about the Galilean," Simon confided. "All these reports of different kinds of healing, all these stories of the miracles that he performs—they have convinced me that I would be a fool not to at least meet him."

Lazarus sat back on his heels. "Have you told Martha of your change of mind?"

"No."

"Why not?"

"Does a man have to tell his wife everything?"

"No, but this—"

"If this doesn't work, she will be more disillusioned

than ever. I don't want her to know until I am healed."
There was a long pause.

Lazarus waited, not agreeing with Simon's reasoning,
not even certain that he understood it. But, at the same
time, he feared that to argue about it would turn Simon
away completely.

"You must keep my confidence, Lazarus," Simon finally said. "Will you?"

"I will keep your confidence, brother-in-law."

"Will you take me to Galilee to find Jesus?"

"I will. But how will we keep that from Martha?"

"We will tell her, and Mary, that we are going to
the Dead Sea to gather chrysolites; that we need such
gemstones for signets we are making for Herod's min-
isters."

With a laugh Lazarus turned around and sat down on
the ground. "You sound as if you've been planning this
for some time, Simon."

"I have," Simon chuckled. "For Martha, we need a
complete plan. Her questions can be as entangling as
briars."

"You realize we'll have to come home with a supply
of chrysolites to make your plan complete."

"I do."

"The Dead Sea is the wrong way to get to Galilee.
And we can't go both places. I can't be gone from the
shop forever!"

"We'll send Bulla to get the chrysolites."

"And who will we leave in charge of the shop?"

"Stefan."

Lazarus shook his head. "Leave Bulla in charge. Send
Stefan to the Dead Sea."

And so it was arranged for Stefan to gather chrysolites

at the mines near the Dead Sea and return with them to the shop in Jerusalem. Bulla was left in charge of the shop, knowing only that Lazarus was making a business trip to Galilee and that he was taking Simon with him. He was cautioned to say nothing to Martha, Mary, or any of the household servants about any of these convoluted arrangements.

"Simon, it would be so much simpler if we just told Martha where we're going and why!" Lazarus protested at one point.

"I will not build up her hopes!" came the adamant reply. "We either do it my way or we don't do it at all."

And so it was that Lazarus and Simon set off early one morning going eastward along the Jericho road, as if on their way to the mines near the Dead Sea. Lazarus had bought horses for the trip from the Romans, having asked the centurion Delos Marcus to negotiate the purchase for him. As a result, he and Simon now owned two well-trained, easy-riding animals with all the necessary livery for a quite reasonable price.

"That Roman will ask you for a favor someday in repayment," Simon warned when told how little the animals cost.

"You are a skeptic, Simon," Lazarus laughed. "Enjoy the ride. It's better than walking to Galilee."

Riding made the trip much faster. By late morning, they had passed Jericho and reached the fording place of the Jordan where they had come seeking Simon's healing from John the Baptizer. On this day they did not pause but crossed to the eastern shore and trailed northward through Perea. At the place where they had camped overnight on the trip to Cana, Lazarus called a halt.

Simon, in obvious fatigue, dismounted without argument.

"There is firewood close by, my brother. If you will, gather some."

Simon nodded and went to look for it while Lazarus led the horses to the river to drink and then tethered them close to nearby forage. They both finished their chores about the same time, laid the fire, and set it blazing against the chill of the night.

They ate from packets of food Martha and Mary had prepared for them; and then, pulling their cloaks close about them, stretched out full length on the ground near the fire.

It seemed to Lazarus that dawn hurried itself, and he was glad. He had slept fitfully, turning often, trying to find a softer spot in the Perean landscape on which to rest and comfort his body. He sat up at the first faint light and called to Simon on the other side of the now-lifeless campfire. The older man roused quickly. He, too, had found no soft spot on which to sleep.

"By the time we sleep again, my brother," Lazarus said, "we will be in Galilee. Very near Amaathus, I should imagine."

"How hard will it be to find Jesus?"

"If the reports are true about the crowds he has following him, it should not be hard at all. We will inquire about him in Amaathus."

Friends in Amaathus did, in fact, know where Jesus was preaching. "In the hills. Near Capernaum," they reported.

"Good. That's where four of Jesus' men live," Lazarus said. "They'll certainly know where he is."

Simon looked at him with surprise. "How do you know these men?"

"We met them at the wedding in Cana."

And so Lazarus and Simon set out northward along the shore of the Sea of Galilee. They passed through the villages of Magdala and Gennesaret then, continuing to follow the shoreline, angled eastward toward Capernaum. As they neared the village of fishermen, they saw a great multitude of people coming down from the hills.

"What is all of this?" Simon exclaimed.

"They must be following Jesus," Lazarus said, excitement in his voice. "Who else could attract such a following?"

"Let's wait here, until they have dispersed," Simon said, reining in his horse, unwilling to get into a crowd because of his disease.

Lazarus nodded in understanding and followed Simon toward a shaded area near the shoreline. There they rested the horses, ate a simple meal, and waited.

As the sun lowered itself behind a ridge of hills, the crowd appeared to have gone away. Lazarus suggested they now go on into Capernaum and find Jesus. Simon agreed, and they continued the last short distance of their journey. Once inside the village Lazarus inquired for the location of the house of John's and James's father, Zebedee, and were directed toward a large compound situated quite near the shore. Just beyond the compound several fishing boats were pulled up at a short wooden quay and some were anchored in the nearby shallows.

"Fishermen! How do they ever stand the smell of their trade?" Simon growled.

"The same way we stand the heat of the smelter and the acrid smell of the metals we work with," Lazarus said laughing. "They get used to it!"

At the gate to the compound they dismounted and tethered the horses. They started to knock at the gate when Lazarus saw Jesus coming toward them from a different direction. "There is Jesus, Simon." He pointed and waved.

Jesus returned the greeting.

Simon stopped, his rebellious spirit startled by the sight of Jesus.

Misreading his brother-in-law's reaction, Lazarus said, "The two men with Jesus are James and John. Do not be afraid."

Simon did not move.

"Go to him, Simon. Speak to him," Lazarus urged.

Uncertainty ridged Simon's forehead.

"You must ask him to help you, Simon."

Simon seemed not to hear.

Jesus slowed and motioned for John and James to stop.

Simon stared, his rebellious spirit afraid in the presence of Jesus' powerful calmness.

"You must ask him to help you, Simon," Lazarus repeated.

Jesus came forward another step or two and waited.

A tremor went through Simon. Rebellion faded to reluctance. Reluctance gave way to the greater need of healing. Tears of surrender poured from his eyes. He dropped to his knees and said, "Lord, if you will, you can make me clean."

The words came forth as a great sobbing plea, which

revealed the depth of his misery and his shame. Revealed too, was the vulnerability and the fear he had so carefully hidden under a mask of harshness.

A look of compassion filled Jesus' face.

Simon saw it and trembled again at the flash of understanding that swept over him. The power of Jesus' compassion had overwhelmed, yet undergirded his spirit. It had demanded of him a confession of weakness and surrender. At the same time, Jesus accepted the confession without judgment or condemnation. It was an expression of a kind of love he never knew existed.

Jesus put forth his hand and touched Simon's forehead. "I will. You are clean!"

Simon straightened and stood up. "I feel clean and whole."

Jesus motioned for Lazarus to come forward and behold his brother-in-law devoid of disease, cleansed of leprosy.

"How can I thank you?" Simon wanted to know. "How can I ever thank you enough?"

"Go your way. Show yourself to the priests in Jerusalem," Jesus said. "Offer the gift that Moses commanded as a testimony to them. But see that you tell no one else of this."

8

IN spite of the fact that Jesus asked him to tell no one about his healing, Simon found himself simply incapable of such secrecy. The joy was too great, the healing too pure, the relief and gratitude too vibrant. His heart sang with the enormous wonder of it, and his lips had to bear witness to Jesus' great power.

James and John, of course, had witnessed the miracle for themselves. They told of it to their father's household when they introduced Simon and Lazarus as their overnight guests immediately following the great incident.

But the next morning when Simon and Lazarus were traveling back to their home in Bethany, Simon's urge to witness could not be denied. On the road between Magdala and Tiberias, they were stopped by a Roman centurion and his squad for questioning about their horses. Lazarus explained they had been purchased.

The centurion walked between the horses and grasped the reins of both. In a stern, unyielding voice, he asked, "You have a bill of sale?"

Lazarus nodded, reached into the folds of his robe,

pulled forth his money pouch, and drew from it the bit of parchment that recorded his ownership of the animals and their livery.

The centurion looked carefully at the parchment. "The centurion Delos Marcus whose seal is on this, is he known to you personally?"

"He is," Lazarus replied.

"What does he look like?" the centurion pursued.

Lazarus described his Roman friend.

"How is it you know Delos Marcus?"

"He is a customer of our shop from time to time." He turned and indicated Simon. "My brother-in-law and I are silversmiths and workers in metals. We have a shop in Jerusalem."

"We do work for the Romans garrisoned in Jerusalem," Simon spoke up unexpectedly. "Is Delos Marcus a friend of yours, too?"

"He is, sir. A very good friend. That is why I stopped you. I recognized the trappings your horses are wearing as being those belonging to my friend Delos Marcus."

"You wondered what a pair of wandering Jews were doing with Roman horses, eh?" Simon said in a blunt, good-natured way.

The centurion reddened. "In all truth, I did, sir."

Simon chuckled. "What is your name, Roman?"

The centurion removed his helmet and gave a short bow. "My name is Cornelius. Cornelius of Corinth. I am garrisoned at Tiberias."

"We shall be glad to tell Delos Marcus what a good friend he has in you," Lazarus said.

"I will appreciate that." Cornelius let go of the reins and stepped aside. "Are you on your way to Jerusalem now?"

Lazarus nodded.

"You may find the short route through Samaria an easier road to travel now."

"That's odd," Lazarus said. "We've always been told it is unsafe for Jews to travel through Samaria."

"It always has been," Cornelius admitted. "And it may still be. But certainly it will be faster traveling that way. The road through Perea is jammed with pilgrims who are coming into Galilee looking for that Galilean preacher."

Lazarus and Simon exchanged looks of caution.

Misreading the looks, Cornelius hurriedly explained. "Surely you've heard of him. His name is Jesus. Jesus of Nazareth. You have heard of him, haven't you?"

Their moment of hesitation spurred the Roman to further explanation. "He is different from any other preacher, I am told. And it is said that he heals. But of course, that is a hard thing to believe, isn't it?"

Before Lazarus could stop him, Simon dismounted, threw back the hood of his robe so that the clear, fresh, healthiness of his face and neck was visible to all. "Hard to believe or not, the power of Jesus' healing is real. I stand before you as proof of it."

Confusion stirred among the squad of soldiers.

Simon walked toward Cornelius. "I have been healed of leprosy by the preacher Jesus."

Murmurs of disbelief came from the soldiers.

Cornelius stared at him, trying to understand the full meaning of his words.

"Simon!" Lazarus reminded him, "You are to say nothing."

"I must! This man must know of Jesus' great power. He and his men need to know how real it is!"

Cornelius continued to stare at him.

Simon held out his hands, clear, clean, still white since the bandages had been removed so recently. "These craftsman's hands have been idle for many, many months because of that foul disease. But look at them now! They once more will be useful hands, working hands, healed by the power of Jesus of Nazareth!"

"Go and find him, Roman!" Lazarus urged. "From the look on your face, you want to believe that he is real. We both can tell you he is."

"But what would he have to do with me? I am a Roman, not a Jew!"

"With Jesus I think it makes no difference," Simon said. "We hear he has healed Gentiles, too."

"I am in your debt," Cornelius bowed to Simon.

Simon bowed and remounted his horse.

Cornelius bade them farewell. "A safe journey to you both."

They rode for a time in silence. A cover of clouds softened the heat and made traveling pleasant and peaceful. They bypassed Tiberias, the city Herod had built atop ancient Jewish graveyards, and without discussion took the road that led directly southward through the hill country of Samaria.

Heaven's covering of clouds increased, darkening the Samaritan landscape, dulling to an even darker green the rich stalks of corn stretching into the distance. By the time they approached Jacob's Well just outside the village of Sychar, the day was deepening to twilight. At the well was a goatherd and here and there travelers like themselves.

"The horses will welcome water as much as we will," Lazarus said, reining to a halt, dismounting and leading his horse carefully through the herd of goats toward the watering place.

Simon, too, dismounted and followed him. "I'd also welcome food, my brother."

"We have nothing but bread left."

"The goatherd might have cheese to sell."

"That he might."

Simon approached the man, inquiring about the cheese, and found him willing to sell some.

"You have come from a long distance?" the goatherd asked, pocketing the coins Simon paid him.

"From Capernaum in Galilee."

The man peered hard at Simon through the deepening twilight.

Simon pulled back in annoyance. "Are you blind?"

The man shook his head. "But you have been."

"What do you mean?"

"You have been healed of leprosy, haven't you?"

Lazarus overheard and came to join the astonished Simon. "How do you know of such things?"

"One other time I saw this same clear, fresh look of new health in a man's face."

"Where?"

"Just beyond Jordan."

"But how? Who?"

"I don't know how. I only know it was the rabbi Jesus who healed a leper from Scythopolis. Did the same rabbi heal you?"

Lazarus and Simon were stunned and silent.

The goatherd shrugged, made a clicking sound with his tongue, calling the goats to him, and herded them off westward on the road to Sychar and Shechem.

"My healing shows even when I don't mention it!"

"We must go straight to the priests at the Temple and make a sacrifice as Jesus told you to do," Lazarus reminded him.

They finished watering their horses and moved away from the well to make room for other travelers. Down the road a short distance, they found a suitable place to eat and rest.

"This cheese has an odd smell to it," Lazarus said, wrinkling his nose. He nibbled at it. "And it has an even odder taste." He put it aside, broke off a piece of the crusty brown bread, and ate it instead.

Simon did not seem to mind the smell or the taste of the cheese and soon finished Lazarus's portion, as well as his own.

"I long for the taste of Martha's good cooking," Lazarus said in a quiet voice. "And I long for my own bed."

"And I'm eager to show Martha my healed body!" Simon exclaimed. "Can't you just imagine her surprise when she sees that I am healed! Completely healed!"

"She will be speechless," Lazarus agreed. "Her faith will be confirmed."

"Yes," Simon said, thoughtfully. "It was my day of good fortune when I chose her for my wife."

"Since we're both so eager for our home, let's travel on tonight, my brother. If we do, we'll be in Jerusalem in time for the morning sacrifice at the Temple and then home by midmorning."

"Travel at night? Through Samaria?"

"Why not?"

"It's too dangerous."

"We have nothing of value on us. No jewels. Very little money."

"It's still too dangerous."

"The Lord would not have healed you just to let you become a victim of road bandits," Lazarus chided. "Let's travel on."

With reluctance Simon agreed, wrapped the remainder of the bread and cheese into two small packets, shoved them inside his waist sash, and remounted his horse.

They rode in the silence of the night with only the snuffle of horses and the creak of saddles interrupting. Heaven's canopy was star-studded, diamondlike in brilliance, and seemed close enough to be touched and cherished by a craftsman's fingertips.

"I would like to create something rare and precious to give to Jesus," Simon said suddenly, raising a hand as if to gather in the stars. "I must find some way to thank him."

"He told you how to do that. By making a sacrifice at the Temple. By telling the priests about your healing."

"But I must find some other way, too. I must find some way to thank him personally."

By the time they reached Jerusalem, dawn streaked the eastern sky. They rode directly to the Sheep Market, purchased a fine, pure white ewe, and made their way toward the Temple Mount. They stabled the horses near their own shop and went the rest of the way on foot, leading the ewe by a strand of rope.

Once inside the Court of Israel, Simon found a priest, told him he wished to make a sacrifice and to issue up prayers of thanksgiving for a healing, and handed the ewe over to him.

The priest merely nodded and led the ewe forward toward the altar, where other priests were slaughtering sacrificial animals and carefully gathering their blood in silver bowls from which it would be spattered against the altar as prayers were intoned.

"Didn't he hear you, Simon?" Lazarus spoke loudly over the noise of the crowd around them. "Or is it that he has no understanding of the miracle you received."

"Unless he is deaf, he is a man hard to impress," Simon replied, looking about for a way to shove through the crowd and follow the priest.

"Forgive me, sir." It was a man close by who spoke. "Did I hear you tell the priest you had received a miracle healing?"

Simon and Lazarus turned at the same time. The man who spoke was of medium height and portly. His beard and mustache were white and neatly trimmed. His eyebrows were thick and white, as were the straggles of hair visible beneath his turban. His eyes were the color of amber, matching the signet he wore about his neck, and his robes were made of rich fabric.

"It is as you say," Simon confirmed.

A light of interest sparked in the man's eyes.

Two other men nearby stopped talking and turned to listen.

"I came here to offer a sacrifice of praise and thanksgiving for this miracle," Simon said.

"But the priest seems unimpressed," Lazarus added.

"Tell me," the man asked, "how and where was this miracle performed?"

"In Galilee. At Capernaum."

The man's look of interest intensified. "Who performed the miracle?"

"Jesus of Nazareth."

A peculiar smile gripped the corners of his mouth in such a way that Simon and Lazarus realized he was neither surprised at hearing Jesus' name nor antagonized by it.

"You know Jesus?" Simon asked, noticing that several men were now listening to the conversation, openly curious.

"Only by reputation."

A murmur went among the other men.

"You should meet him personally," Lazarus said. "He is a most different kind of man."

Someone laughed.

Another made a scornful sound.

And yet a third man said, "No wonder the priest turned a deaf ear to your story of a miracle."

The white-bearded man frowned, stepped closer to Simon, touched his arm, and motioned that they should walk away from the intruders.

When Simon and Lazarus began to follow, someone called out, "Take care, Joseph of Arimathea, lest your Sanhedrin brothers accuse you of heresy, too!"

"You are Joseph of Arimathea?" an astonished Lazarus asked as they passed through the gateway and walked toward the roofed area of the Temple Mount called the Porches of Solomon. "I know of you, merchant. It is said of you that you are reasonable and fair."

"My heart thanks you for such a compliment."

"We have purchased stones and metals from your caravans on many occasions," Simon said. "We know that you are reasonable and fair in trading."

"My money pouch thanks you, too." Joseph laughed. "What are your names?"

When they introduced themselves and their shop, Joseph nodded in obvious recognition. "It was you who created the crown for the Lady Herodias, wasn't it?"

"You know of that?" Lazarus asked in surprise.

"Everyone in Herod's tetrarchy knows of it!" came the amused reply.

"Even the Romans?"

"Even the Romans. They think of it as a joke." He turned to Simon. A look of seriousness replaced his amusement. "But please, if I may intrude into your personal life, it is your experience with Jesus that interests me."

"You, too, have need of healing?"

Joseph shook his head. "I want to know all about your healing, sir."

Simon told his story from the beginning. He left out nothing—Martha's insistence that he could be healed by faith, his resistance, Lazarus's bringing Jesus to their house, his refusal even to meet him, the apparent remission of the disease after Jesus' visit, Martha's crediting Jesus' healing power, more and more stories about Jesus being brought by friends and neighbors, his own change of heart about Jesus. "And so it was that I asked Lazarus to take me to Galilee to find Jesus. He did so. We met Jesus at the house of Zebedee the fisherman in Capernaum. The sons of Zebedee, James and John, are close followers of Jesus."

"And did you ask Jesus for healing?"

"I did."

"And?"

"It occurred. Then and there. It was as if a great burden was lifted from me, and I have never felt such peace in my spirit. Never before have I felt such peace."

"What was your disease?"

"Leprosy."

The intensity with which Joseph of Arimathea had listened to his entire story did not abate. He did not step away, nor did he show any fear or surprise.

Simon pushed back the hood of his robe to reveal his head and face; then he held out his hands to show that they, too, were free of blemish or disease. "It is the healing power of Jesus that has created this," Simon said matter-of-factly. "The power is his. The credit is his."

Slowly, thoughtfully, the merchant nodded.

"He deserves our deepest respect," Lazarus added.

"I agree. But he will not receive it from the Sanhedrin, I fear. Nor from the priesthood."

Simon replaced the hood of his robe over his head. "They will fight him out of jealousy, won't they?"

The merchant nodded.

"Can't you persuade them otherwise?"

"I will try. But who can say what the outcome will be?"

9

WHEN Simon and Lazarus finally arrived home in Bethany, Martha was the first to see them coming. She ran from the house to meet them.

Simon stopped in the shade of the great almond tree, threw off the hood of his robe, and watched hungrily for her reaction.

She halted a few feet from him, her eyes searching his head and face for the awful sores. When she realized they were gone, a crooked, funny look shattered across her face. She clasped her hands together in a prayerful gesture, stifled the cry of joy that sprang to her lips, and in the next moment was on her knees, tears streaming from her eyes.

Simon went to her, knelt, embraced her, held her close. Gently he began to rock back and forth as he might do to comfort a small child.

The tenderness was unexpected. Lazarus glanced away, fought down the lump rising in his throat, and walked quietly past them toward the house to find Mary and tell her of the miracle.

"It is as you said it would be, my wife," Simon whispered. "Jesus has healed me."

She brushed at her tears with the back of her hand, and looked up at him. "And you told me you were going to dig for chrysolites!"

He chuckled. "But I have returned with a much more valuable gift than any gemstone!"

She reached out, touched his face with trembling fingers, and began once more to cry.

Simon brought forth a small square of cotton from the folds of his robe and began to dab at the fresh tears.

She took the cotton square from him. "We must do something special for Jesus," she said, getting up onto her feet. "We must find a way to thank him personally."

Simon got up, too. "That's what I told Lazarus on the way home from Galilee. We have done what Jesus told us. We went to the Temple and made a sacrifice of thanksgiving. We told the priest about what Jesus had done, but . . ."

"But what?"

"The priest seemed unimpressed."

Martha frowned. "That's the way the priests were each time Mary and I prayed for your healing and gave sacrifices. The priests were uninterested. I thought it was because we were just women."

He took hold of her arm and guided her toward the house. "The only person who even seemed to believe me was the merchant Joseph of Arimathea."

"He is a wise and a just man, isn't he?"

Simon nodded. "He thinks Jesus is in danger from the Sanhedrin, and from the priesthood."

Martha stopped abruptly and turned to him. "Danger?"

"Danger. Joseph says they fear Jesus. That makes him dangerous. And it puts him in danger."

"Then we shall have to help Jesus any way we can."

"It means that whoever helps him also will be in danger," Simon reminded her.

"There can be no greater danger than that which Jesus has helped you to pass through," she said quietly. "We shall have to be ready at all times to shelter and feed Jesus. That is the very least we can do for him."

"And his men, too." Simon added.

She nodded.

"There are twelve of them now."

"Twelve?"

"It will require much more work for you when they come to stay with us."

"It will be worth it," she said, turning and touching his face once more.

He smiled and led her into the house, where Mary, Lazarus, and all the servants stood waiting for them. A great shout of jubilation went up as they entered the room.

Mary ran to him, flung her arms about him in an embrace of joy. The servants were alternately grinning and crying, and then, one by one, they pressed forward to shake his hand and make personal expressions of their delight at his healing.

Breathless from the excitement of it all, he finally held both hands high, thanking them for the greetings, and urging them to bring an end to the tumultuous home-coming.

"We're hungry," Lazarus announced. "Is there food in this house?"

"There is always food in this house," Martha laughed,

turning toward the cooking area. The servants turned away and went back to their chores. "Come along, Mary. Let us set a feast before these two hungry men."

The jubilation and good feelings lasted for weeks. Simon never thought to tell Martha, or anyone else, about Jesus' admonition to not talk about the miracle. Household servants told servants of other households. Servants told masters and mistresses. Neighbors thronged into Martha's garden and house to see Simon for themselves. They brought relatives and friends. Even strangers, having heard of the miraculous healing, came to stand in the road or lean against the rock fence to stare at the house where Simon lived. Martha turned no one away.

Nor did Simon. He resumed an active role in the running of the shop in Jerusalem. Every tradesman that did business with the shop was told about the miracle. Always Jesus was given full credit for the power and the reality of it all.

"I am proud for your miracle, Simon," Bulla said on the first day he returned to the shop. "But you may have to turn away some of these people."

"Why should I?" Simon asked in surprise.

"Because while you and Lazarus were in Galilee, Herod Antipas sent Chuza to us with another large order."

"What does Herod want now? Another crown?" Simon asked with a laugh, winking at Lazarus.

Bulla shook his head. "Herod wants a new design for the signets worn by members of his royal household."

"What's wrong with the one they have?"

"It is too easily copied by those who have no right to wear or use such an important seal."

And so while Lazarus set about designing a new royal signet, Simon set about purchasing more raw materials, hiring more craftsmen, and overseeing production. His energy was now as limitless as his enthusiasm. He continued to tell of his healing to any and all who asked. Jesus' admonition to tell no one was forgotten.

But the effects of Simon's healing on Martha and Mary could not be forgotten. Martha was much more affectionate and loving to the family. She now spoke gently to the servants.

"The awful burden of worry has been lifted from her," Zoë explained to a neighbor's servant. "She has always been a kind woman. It just shows more now."

It was true. Martha seemed more contented and at peace with herself. Always hospitable, she now spent even more time visiting with Timora and other neighbors. She was among the first to help when a need arose. And she no longer complained about Mary's daydreaming and solitary meditations. Before Simon's healing, she fussed loudly at it; she often accused Mary of wasting time or badgered her for not being as helpful as she should be with managing the household. She now seemed to find Mary's prayers and meditations important.

For her part, Mary welcomed the newfound freedom to be as solitary and contemplative as she liked. But from these periods of reflection and meditation, she began to be aware of a burden to do something more by way of thanking Jesus. She knew, of course, that Simon and Lazarus had made a sacrifice of thanksgiving on their return from Galilee. Lazarus had told her about it. But she wanted to do something herself. She began to urge Lazarus to take her with him to the Temple to make a praise offering.

Finally, in spite of all the work he had to do at the

shop, he agreed. And on a bright autumn morning, a few days before the Feast of Shelters, Mary accompanied Lazarus and Simon on their way to work in Jerusalem. At the foot of the Temple Mount near the Huldah Gate, Simon bade them farewell and went on to the shop.

Lazarus led Mary up the steps and through the great triple gates into the area where the money changers had their booths and where merchants sold sacrificial animals and doves to pilgrims and worshipers. The place was crowded and noisy. He stopped at the first booth he could find where the purest of pure white sheep were sold. But before he could begin bargaining with the boothkeeper, Mary tugged at his sleeve. He glanced around at her.

She shook her head, leaned toward him and whispered, "Not a sheep, my brother. Not a sheep. A dove, if you please."

"But a sheep is a much more impressive sacrifice!"

She shook her head again. "A dove, if you please."

He sighed, shrugged apologetically to the boothkeeper, and led Mary down the rows of booths until they came to a seller of doves.

Mary carefully searched the reed cages for just the right bird.

"Any one of those will do, won't it?" Lazarus urged, impatient to get to the shop.

"It must be exactly the right one," she answered placidly. "It must look like the one I saw before."

"Saw? Before? Where before?"

"At the Jordan. At the baptism." She went around to the side of the stacked cages, still carefully inspecting each dove, and at last pointed to one on the very bottom of one stack and turned to the dove merchant. "This one, I think. May I see it more closely?"

He looked chagrined, obviously not wanting to move

all the cages, and tried to interest her in another by pointing to the cage that was easiest to reach.

Mary smiled, shook her head, and pointed again to the cage at the bottom of the stack.

The dove merchant glanced at Lazarus. "You have no authority over your wife?"

"She is not my wife. She is my sister," Lazarus retorted, as impatient with the merchant as with Mary's insistence on a particular dove. "Show her the dove she wants."

The merchant muttered something under his breath, unstacked the cages, and handed Mary the cage.

The dove inside was pure white. It did not flutter about or seem frightened when its cage was moved.

To Lazarus it looked no different from a dozen of the other doves the merchant had for sale.

But for Mary there was obviously something different about this one. She slowly turned the cage around and around, inspecting the dove from every angle. Finally satisfied, she smiled again at the merchant and at Lazarus. "This one is the one I want you to buy, please."

Lazarus paid the merchant his asking price without even bothering to haggle and hurried Mary on up the wide inner stairway leading to the Temple Mount.

The top of the stairway opened out onto the Porches of Solomon. Deep shade lay beneath the elaborate peristyle. Crowds of people were already gathered. Beyond the shade, across the wide expanse of the Court of Gentiles, rose the glistening prominence of the Temple itself. The morning sunlight dazzled from its white marble and gold ornaments.

Mary shielded her eyes and handed the dove in its

cage to Lazarus. "I will pray in the Women's Court while you find a priest to make the sacrifice."

"I will pray, too," he agreed.

Mary turned into the Women's Court, bypassed the crowded forepart of the area, and went to the stone bench near the back. Only two other women were there. They sat heavily shawled and with heads bowed in prayer.

Mary sat down a distance from them, unloosed her veil, and pushed aside her head shawl. "O Lord," she said, looking skyward. "I am your servant, Mary of Bethany. Behold the thankful heart I bring to your holy Temple." She spoke very softly so as not to disturb the others. "I thank you for the healing powers of your gracious son, Jesus. He has shared those powers in behalf of my brother-in-law, Simon of Bethany."

She closed her eyes against an increasing brilliance emanating from the Temple, and reenvisioned the miracle of the dove descending on Jesus at the River Jordan. "I praise your holy name, O Lord, and give thanks to you for your wonderful mercy through a sacrificial dove. As it is written, so shall it be done."

She sat quietly then, envisioning again and again and again the miracle of the dove descending on Jesus, reliving the indescribable joy that the sight of it had brought to her, cherishing the wonder and the majesty of it, until at last tears of joy and thanksgiving blurred the images of remembrance.

At the other end of the stone bench, one of the heavily shawled women got up and left.

Mary stirred, unaware of how long she had meditated. The morning sunlight still reflected brilliantly from the face of the Temple but now was distorted by intervening waves of heat issuing up from the stone flooring of the court. Crowd noises from the Court of the Gentiles invaded the delicate quiet that had prevailed before.

She looked toward the gate and saw an impatient Lazarus motioning for her to come. Quickly she replaced her head shawl and went to him. By the time she reached him, he was busy in conversation.

"Mary, look who is here in Jerusalem," Lazarus said. "It's our friend Levi that we met in Cana."

"Of course," she said, recalling him—most particularly the friendly interest he had shown toward her.

"Only now you must call me by a different name. You must call me Matthew."

"Matthew?"

He smiled broadly and nodded. "I have been renamed. By the Master."

"The Master?"

"Jesus, Mary," Lazarus said. "Jesus is the master he refers to!"

Mary looked at him with altered interest. How could a tax collector be one of Jesus' men?

Matthew grinned at her and nodded enthusiastically. "It is true. I am one of Jesus' men now. In fact, I am here in Jerusalem trying to make arrangements for our lodging during the Feast of Shelters. But I am finding that the landlords have raised their prices until . . ."

Mary, looking at Lazarus, interrupted. "Why should they have to stay here in Jerusalem? Why don't you invite them to stay at our house, my brother?"

A startled look came onto Matthew's face. He started to protest.

Lazarus's face lighted up. "Of course. I should have

thought of that! As Mary has said, come and stay at our place over in Bethany."

"I feel like I have forced the invitation," Matthew said.

"Please, don't feel that way," Mary said, turning to him. "Jesus has done much for us. He has healed Simon. We insist that you come to our house."

Still Matthew hesitated. "There will be twelve of us. And the Master said not to inconvenience anyone."

"All the more reason you should come to our place," Mary urged. "We have the room for you."

Matthew looked deep into her eyes and then without further hesitation nodded his acceptance.

"Good! Then it's all settled," Lazarus said happily. "Mary will show you the way to our house. I must get on to my shop. You understand."

They said farewell on the street at the foot of the steps to the Huldah Gate. Lazarus went northward through the winding Street of Bazaars toward his shop.

Mary and Matthew went eastward, leaving the city through the Lion's Gate, and onto the road that led down through the Kidron Valley, up and across the Mount of Olives, and into the village of Bethany.

The autumn afternoon was sunny and warm, the journey pleasant. They walked together in companionable silence until Mary's curiosity about Jesus' men unloosed her tongue.

"Tell me about Jesus' men, Matthew. Tell me what your brothers are like," she said.

"In Cana you met the four who are the closest to Jesus," he reminded her. "Peter, Andrew, James, and John have known him the longest. James and John are even related to him. Their mothers are sisters."

Mary glanced at him in surprise. "But Jesus seems to stand so apart."

Matthew agreed. "There is a presence about him that I have not sensed with any other man."

They walked on a while in silence again, each considering what it was that made Jesus such a different person. A small breeze riffled around them. A young boy approached herding a small flock of sheep. They stepped aside and waited for him to pass.

"What of the others?" Mary asked as they once more moved up the slope of the Mount of Olives.

"There is Philip. I think of him as Philip the cautious. He takes his time about things. And there is Nathanael, whose real name is Bartholomew. Jesus chose to give him a different name, too."

"And what is he like?"

Matthew slowed his pace and looked carefully at Mary. "I would say, in a way, that he is like you, Mary."

She laughed and ducked her head, thinking he was teasing her.

"Oh, I'm quite serious," he protested. "Really, quite serious. For I would call Nathanael a guileless person."

"Guileless?"

He nodded. "Guileless. A person of meditation. A person of devotion. You are a person like that, aren't you?"

She did not answer.

Amused at her shyness, he went on. "Then, of course, there is Thomas, the doubter. He always questions everything and everybody. And Thaddeus, a warm-hearted man who, along with James the Less, is helpful to all, and most faithful.

"Simon the Zealot, of course, is a man of fervor who

helps to lead many to the Master. And he also helps to lead many away from the Master, he's such an impassioned, definite person."

"That's ten," Mary said. "You, of course, make the eleventh, but who is the twelfth?"

"Ah," Matthew's faced darkened a bit with uncertainty. "The twelfth of the Master's men is named Judas. We call him Judas Iscariot since he comes from the area near Keriot."

"Why do you frown when you speak of him?"

Matthew looked perplexed and shook his head. "There is something about him—I don't know what—but something that causes me to feel cautious." He was thoughtful for a moment, then brightened and gave a small laugh. "Perhaps it is because he, too, handles money. He is the treasurer for the twelve of us. Maybe my caution comes from the fact that, as a former tax collector, I miss the feel of money!"

She smiled at him, appreciating his humor. She decided that she liked him and wondered if he was married.

"Why do you ask about Jesus' men?"

"To better understand Jesus, I think," she replied. "Was it hard for you to join his men?"

"No, it wasn't." His answer came without hesitation.

Again she wondered if he was married, and if he had given up his wife to join Jesus. She had found him so easy to talk to about the others, she considered asking him about himself.

At the crest of the Mount of Olives, they stopped. Below them, not far away, was the village of Bethany, its cluster of houses shining in the early afternoon sun. Near many of the houses were great shade trees and gardens of vegetables and grapevines, and beyond these were groves of olive trees intermingling with the taller date palms.

"Which is your house?" Matthew asked.

She pointed to the largest one in the village. It was a compound surrounded by gardens and partially sheltered by the great almond tree near the front gate. They moved on, this time at a faster pace going down the slope toward the house.

When they arrived, Martha greeted them warmly, and when Mary told her about inviting Jesus' men to stay at the house, her cordiality turned to enthusiasm. "Will Jesus, too, be with you?" she asked.

Matthew shook his head. "The Master says it is not yet the right time for him to come."

Mary looked disappointed.

But Martha nodded as if expecting such an answer. "Simon has told me something about the rising danger for Jesus in Jerusalem."

"Danger? We know of no danger for him," Matthew said. "In fact, all of us who are close to him urged him to come. John even pointed out that if he wants to be known publicly, he must reveal himself."

Martha brought cups of cool water to them both, and urged them to rest in the shade of the great almond tree.

Matthew drank deeply from the cup and returned it with a nod of thanks. "Danger, you say?"

"Danger, indeed," Martha replied. "But you can discuss it further with Simon."

Matthew held up a hand, as if something in his memory fit with the word *danger*. "I wonder . . ."

"What?" Mary asked.

A look of deep concentration came on Matthew's face. He stood up and paced a bit. "It was something Jesus said about it not being the right time for him to come to the festival."

"The right time? What caused him to think that?" Mary asked.

"Then he is aware of the danger that Simon speaks of." Martha's tone was one of certainty.

Matthew started to protest but apparently thought better of it and instead said, "Jesus isn't coming, anyway. So whatever the danger, it will no doubt pass."

10

"TELL us again, my mistress," Zoë said. "What are the words that are written in the great Torah?"

"You mean about the festival?"

"Yes, mistress."

Martha picked up another twig of myrtle and thought for a moment. "You shall observe the Feast of Shelters for seven days after you have gathered in the corn and the wine."

"And does it also say we are to build a large booth, mistress?" asked the young orphan boy named Mimne who had been with them for several years.

"I think it does, Mimne. That's how we know to build the booths of twigs of myrtle and willow and palm."

"And it's how we know to make lulavs," said Zoë. "The celebration wouldn't be complete without those festal plumes."

"I'm glad that Jesus' men are coming again," Mimne said.

"So am I, lad, so am I. Go now and bring more willow

branches. I want this booth finished by the time they arrive. There's still a lot to do."

She watched him go, thinking how glad she was they had taken him in, and how glad she was that the Feast of Shelters was such a grand celebration of happiness and thanksgiving. This year they were thankful for more than just the fine harvests.

With Simon's healing, it would a time of real merriment and laughter, singing and music and dancing.

Jesus' men arrived a few hours later and for the next seven days were in and out of the house, coming and going into Jerusalem. The Holy City was filigreed with a lacework of new color from the thousands of pilgrims' booths. Many prayers of thanksgiving were rendered up to the bluest of heavens high above the marble and gold Temple.

Many teachers and preachers held forth for the crowds in the Porches of Solomon. They were of particular interest to Jesus' men. On two occasions Martha and Mary went into the Holy City with Matthew, John, and James to offer up their own prayers of thanksgiving for Simon's healing, to show them where Simon and Lazarus's business was located, and to shop for extra vegetables and fruits from the harvest bounty in the bazaars.

On the third day of the festival, about midmorning, after the twelve had gone into Jerusalem again, Jesus came to the house in Bethany.

Zoë saw him coming and ran to find Martha. "The Rabbi from Galilee," she gasped excitedly.

"What about him?"

"He is here, my mistress! He is here."

"Jesus? Here?" Martha untied her apron, threw it aside, and hurried with joy out into the garden.

Overhearing Zoë's announcement, Mary dropped her mending and came quickly from her quiet place at the back of the house.

Jesus stood just inside the gate, waiting to be welcomed, unwilling to force himself on their hospitality.

Martha stretched forth both of her hands, reaching out to him, welcoming him as she would a member of the family.

Smiling broadly, he clasped her hands in his own.

"Come in," she said. "Come in. You have traveled a long way from the looks of you. You must be starving."

He laughed, appreciating her motherly openness.

From behind Martha, Mary made a deep bow, and then stood with head bowed and eyes lowered until he went to her. "It is good to be here again. It is good to see you both again. I could not go on to the festival without stopping to see you."

"But surely you are staying with us!" Mary exclaimed, searching his face with adoring, pleading eyes.

"Your men are staying with us," Martha said. "They said you were not coming. But, of course, you know you are welcome here!"

Jesus walked to a bench in the shade of the great almond tree and sat down. "True. I told them I would not come. Publicly the right time for me to be in Jerusalem has not come."

"Then the rumors that Simon and Lazarus have been hearing are true?" Martha asked.

Jesus nodded.

Zoë and another servant came from the house with a basin of water for the washing of feet, towels, and a cruet of wine, cups, and a basket of fruit.

Jesus thanked them and then turned again to Martha. "Secretly, of course, privately, I can go to Jerusalem anytime. But not publicly. And with those twelve . . ." He laughed lightly and removed his sandals. "What do you think of my twelve men, Martha?"

"Why, I . . . I . . ."

"You find them hard to describe?" He slipped his feet into the basin of water and gave a sigh of relief. "They represent some part of each of us, some characteristic of all of us. They are good men, sincere and eager to help me. But they have not yet . . ."

A servant came, leaned over and rubbed at his feet.

He acknowledged her thoughtfulness with a quick smile as she dried his feet and put his sandals back on.

"What is it your men have not yet done?" Martha asked.

"They do not yet have full faith in me."

The two sisters looked surprised.

"It's not hard to understand," Jesus explained in their defense, reaching for a piece of fruit from the basket. "The power of the spiritual has yet to touch them personally. As, for instance, it has touched your family."

"We praise you for Simon's healing," Martha said.

He nodded and went on. "They also don't yet understand that the world cannot hate them as it hates me."

Mary's eyes grew wide. "Hate? You?"

"Yes, hate. I give evidence to the world that its ways are evil. My men do not."

"Knowing that there is danger for you," Martha said in her practical way, "why do you insist on going to the festival, even privately?"

"I am called to do it."

"Still and all," Martha said, "I hope you'll speak with Simon before going. Let him tell you what he hears among the people. Lazarus will want to help you, too."

When Simon and Lazarus returned from their shop late in the day and Jesus' men also had returned, they all sat down to eat the evening meal in the booth that had been built in the garden.

But there was no laughter and celebration among them. Instead they talked of what the people were saying about Jesus.

"Members of the Sanhedrin and the priesthood are on the lookout for you," Simon began. "Many of them have come to me asking about you."

"What have you told them?"

"That you have the power to heal. That I am the evidence of it."

Jesus looked at him searchingly. "My admonition for silence was not practical, was it?"

Simon hesitated, then reddened with embarrassment as he recalled the admonition. "I apologize, my Lord. The miracle was too joyous. You deserve credit for such powers."

"My Father deserves the credit. The power is his. And that is what people fear."

Silence fell upon them. Martha and Mary stopped in the midst of serving their guests and glanced at each other.

"There is a great deal of talk about you in the crowds, Master," said Peter.

Jesus looked at him inquiringly.

"Some say you are a good man."

"And some say you lead the people astray." John grinned in a teasing way that amused Jesus.

"Do they say these things openly?" Jesus asked.

All shook their heads. "No," Peter said. "They speak of them quietly and confidentially for fear of the Sanhedrin and the priesthood."

"What of Herod and his men?" Jesus asked again.

"They want no trouble with us Jews," Simon replied. "And the Romans want no riots or civil uprisings."

"It is the Sanhedrin and priesthood who are afraid of you, Jesus," Lazarus said. "They are the ones who provoke whatever rancor is in Herod's heart about your teaching and preaching and healing."

When the Feast of Shelters was half over, Jesus went up to Jerusalem and into the Temple. There, in the Porches of Solomon, he began to teach. The priests were astonished and asked each other how he had learned to read. "He has not been educated. He comes from Galilee. He is a carpenter, and son of a carpenter. How is it that he has learned to read?"

Jesus overheard them and answered: "My teaching is not from myself. It comes from the one who sent me. Anyone who is prepared to do his will, will know whether my teaching is from God or whether I speak on my own account."

A murmur went up from the crowd. His words were those of a man of wisdom; yet they were words that no ordinary man of natural wisdom would have spoken.

"His words presume he has a direct relationship with the Holy One," protested a priest from Emmaus.

"Is that not blasphemy?" asked another.

"When someone speaks on his own account," Jesus continued, "he is seeking honor for himself. But when he is seeking the honor of the person who sent him, then he is true and altogether without dishonesty."

On the Sabbath day at the end of the Feast of Shelters, Jesus and his men again went up to Jerusalem. This time Peter led them to a pool next to the Sheep Pool called Bethesda. It had five porticoes, and under these were crowds of sick people, blind, lame, paralyzed. For an angel went down at a certain season into the pool and troubled the water. Anyone stepping in first after the troubling of the water was healed of whatever disease he had.

"There, Master," Peter said, pointing to a lame man struggling in vain to get to the waters of the pool. "We're told that he has been ill for many years."

John interrupted, "For years he has come here to this pool every day, trying to reach the waters, believing that if he can get into them, he will be healed."

Jesus walked over to the man. "Do you want to be well again?"

"Sir," replied the sick man, "I have no one to put me into the pool when the water is disturbed; and while I am still on the way, someone else gets down there before me."

Jesus said, "Get up, pick up your sleeping mat, and walk around."

The man looked dumbfounded, stared at Jesus, blinked his eyes, and struggled up onto his feet. He picked up his mat and started walking around, ecstatic and healed!

The Pharisees and Sadducees there said to the man, "It is the Sabbath. You're not allowed to carry your sleeping mat."

The man replied, "The man who cured me told me to pick up my mat and walk around."

"Who is the man who said this to you?"

The cured man had no idea who it was, since Jesus and his men had disappeared into the crowd.

After a while Jesus met him again in the Temple and said, "Now you are well again. Do not sin anymore, or something worse may happen to you."

The man went back and told the Pharisees and the Sadducees that it was Jesus who had cured him. He also told them what Jesus had said about sinning no more.

They were incensed that Jesus had done such work on the Sabbath. But they were even more angry that he had told the man to sin no more. "Who is he to tell you such a thing? It sounds like blasphemy!" They set out then to find him, and to upbraid and harass him.

But Jesus and his men had already left the Temple to return to the house in Bethany. During the evening meal the conversation centered on the healing of the lame man. Jesus' men were full of enthusiasm about it.

A bit later Matthew confided to Mary, "The Master makes the miraculous seem like an ordinary occurrence. He is so calm about it all. But, in our eyes, it is a miracle."

"I know," Mary answered. "We feel that way about Simon's healing."

"I fear for him, though," Matthew went on as Martha came up to them.

"Why?" she asked.

"There were some men in the crowd that seemed agitated about it all. I think they would have accosted Jesus if we had not left when we did."

"Now he is in even more danger," Martha said.

The following morning a delegation of five Pharisees approached the house in Bethany.

Martha saw them coming and felt the warning sense of danger intensify in her spirit. Jesus and his men had not yet left the house to go back to Galilee; and Simon and Lazarus had delayed the start of their workday in order to have a final conversation with them all. She knew that the Pharisees were coming to rebuke Jesus for curing the lame man. She called softly for Mary to go and warn all the men while she herself went to the entry gate to stand squarely in the middle of it. Hands on hips, she waited, showing no cordiality whatsoever and blocking the way of the approaching delegation.

"Is this the house of Simon and Lazarus, the silversmiths?" asked the man who appeared to lead the delegation.

Martha instantly disliked him. His eyes were too close set astride a thin, pinched nose. His high, pointed turban was an alternating wrap of red and white cloth above the phylactery he wore on his forehead. His robe, also of red and white, was expensively embroidered. His attitude was disdainful, arrogant.

"May I ask who inquires?" Martha replied.

The man hesitated, as if unaccustomed to seeing a woman act so boldly, and then once again asked his question.

Once again Martha replied, "And you, sir, who are you, and who are these men with you?"

The man's face reddened.

One of his companions stepped forward. "We are representatives of the Sanhedrin. My name is Zepphaniah. This is Hiram. He and I, in fact, all of us, are members of the sect of Pharisees. We have need to talk with Simon, or with Lazarus, the silversmiths."

"I am the wife of Simon and the sister of Lazarus. We were expecting no visitors today."

"Is Simon here?" the man asked.

"Better yet, ask the woman if that Galilean preacher

is here!" snapped the first man. "He is the one with whom we take issue!"

Before Martha could answer, Jesus came up behind her and spoke to the Pharisees. "I am the Galilean preacher you seek. Why do you take issue with me?"

"Why did you tell the lame man to carry his sleeping mat on the Sabbath?" demanded the man in the red and white turban. "It is against the Law!"

"And why do you work on the Sabbath?" asked a second man. "That, too, is against the Law."

"My Father still goes on working, and I am at work, too," Jesus answered.

"Blasphemy!"

"You not only break the Sabbath, you speak of the Holy One as if he were your own father!"

"You think you are his equal?"

"In all truth I tell you, by himself the Son can do nothing. He can only do what he sees the Father doing. And whatever the Father does, the Son does, too. For the Father loves the Son and shows him everything he himself does. And he will show him even greater things than these, works that will astonish you."

"Blasphemy!"

"Treason!"

"Heretic!"

"One work I did, and you are all amazed at it. Moses and the patriarchs ordered you to practice circumcision, and you circumcise on the Sabbath. Now if someone can be circumcised on the Sabbath so that the Law of Moses is not broken, why are you angry with me for making someone completely healthy on the Sabbath?"

The Pharisees looked at one another and gave no answer.

"Do not keep judging according to appearances,"

Jesus admonished them. "Let your judgment be according to what is right."

Still the Pharisees gave no answer.

Jesus turned, kissed Martha on the forehead. "My thanks to you and your household for your hospitality. My men and I are in your debt." He waved farewell to Simon, Lazarus, and Mary, and motioned for his men to come.

They brushed past the delegation of Pharisees.

Mary whispered to Martha, "Will the Pharisees leave now?"

"I hope so. I don't wish to be hospitable to them."

Simon and Lazarus came forward and stepped through the gate into the road to confront the delegation.

Simon spoke. "Men of the Sanhedrin. Some of you are customers of our silversmithing and metalworking shop in Jerusalem. You know us as honorable men, as we know you are honorable. Why do you invade the privacy of our home with such rancor?"

"It is that Nazarene, Simon," said the man in the red and white turban. "He is a heretic. Yet you welcome him into your home!"

"He is my friend, Hiram," Simon answered in a quiet but definite tone. "Beyond that, he healed me of a serious disease."

"Yes, yes," Hiram replied impatiently. "We've all heard all about that so-called healing of yours."

"You sound unbelieving."

"I am! And more than that, I accuse you of harboring a heretic!"

Simon's face reddened.

Lazarus started forward menacingly.

Simon stopped him.

Hiram backed away and said in a threatening tone, "You've not heard the last of this. Either one of you!" He swung around, motioning for the others to follow and went back up the road toward Jerusalem.

"I should have let them come in, shouldn't I?" Martha asked, a worried look on her face.

Simon went to her and put his arm around her shoulder. "You did exactly the right thing, my wife. You tried to protect our friend Jesus."

But in spite of his attempt to endorse her actions, she still felt she'd been too blunt. And beyond all doubt, she knew there would be retaliation for it. Pharisees were known for their unforgiveness.

11

As Martha feared, the Pharisees were unforgiving. Within an hour of their return to Jerusalem, Zepphaniah, Hiram, and the rest of the delegation went to report the incident to the High Priest. They were ushered into his house and told to wait in a small anteroom.

The wait was not a long one, however; and as Caiaphas approached them, the five of them rose to their feet and bowed.

"Zepphaniah, Hiram, greetings," Caiaphas said, nodding to the other three. "Did you find the Nazarene?"

"We did, sir." Hiram said.

"And what did he have to say for himself about breaking the law of the Sabbath?"

"That he was justified."

The high priest's eyebrows arched. "Justified? How justified?"

"Justified by the fact that his father did not stop working on the Sabbath."

"His father? I thought his father, the carpenter of Nazareth, was dead."

Hiram pointed upward. "He meant the Holy One."

"Are you certain?" asked Caiaphas.

Hiram turned to Zepphaniah and the others for confirmation of the truth of his report.

In unison they confirmed what Hiram had said.

"Blasphemy!"

Zepphaniah said, "Beyond the obvious sincerity with which the man speaks, he is dangerous to us, honorable sir."

"Yes, yes," Caiaphas said impatiently, pacing away. "I know the danger involved. The people by the thousands are hearing about him, and following him. I know, this Jesus poses a threat to the very order of things! Yes, yes."

"There must be something we can do to stop him," Hiram exclaimed. "It is not right that he should be allowed to go unpunished for this great sin against the law of the Sabbath."

"Will you go with us to seek help from Herod Antipas?" Zepphaniah asked.

Caiaphas stopped pacing and turned. "Herod is not in Jerusalem. He is at his palace in the Fortress Machaerus on the far side of the Jordan."

"Then let us go there. As a delegation, let us insist that he help us by issuing an arrest warrant."

The high priest's face reddened a bit. "He has already issued an order allowing me to do that very thing."

The faces of the men showed surprise.

"And have you issued the arrest warrant?"

"Not yet."

Hiram frowned in anger.

Zepphaniah stopped him. "With all respect, honorable priest, is there a reason you have not done this?"

"There is."

"May we ask what the reason is?"

Caiaphas had started pacing again and did not answer immediately.

In the far part of the residence, the sound of a chime, delicate and sweet, broke the strained silence in the audience room and momentarily softened the atmosphere.

Caiaphas, wishing to avoid a quarrel, once more turned to them. But instead of telling them the reason why no arrest warrant had been issued for Jesus, he said, "Good sirs of the Sanhedrin, I invite you to go with me to Machaerus, to inform Herod of the Nazarene's latest escapade."

The delegation of Pharisees exchanged questioning looks in a silent poll. Then Hiram said, "We will go with you."

Their arrival at Machaerus was not a welcomed one.

Chuza came to greet them and explained, "His Excellency Herod Antipas is entertaining certain consuls from Rome and the Roman governor of Syria. He cannot be disturbed."

Embarrassed but determined, Caiaphas said, "But the time is now imminent for us to take action against the Nazarene as Herod has already indicated he wanted done."

Chuza made a wry face. "And you have not yet done it?"

"Only now is the time right to do so," Caiaphas explained and went on to describe the latest offense.

"I will take the message to his Excellency," Chuza said. "In the meantime, please enjoy the hospitality of the palace. Jabool will be your host until I can return to you." He motioned for one of the lesser officials of the palace to attend the unexpected guests.

When Chuza did return quite a long time later, he informed the delegation that "Herod Antipas does not wish to be bothered with having to send soldiers to seek out and arrest some itinerant, fanatical rabbi from Galilee."

"Then who will do it?" Caiaphas asked. "There are not enough Temple guards to handle such a duty. Who will do it?"

A distressed look came onto the face of the little round man who had been Herod's minister of finance and household affairs for so many years. He took Caiaphas by the arm, led him to a settee, and sat down with him. "Honorable priest, you and I have been friends for many years, have we not?"

Caiaphas nodded.

"Have I ever misled you?"

Caiaphas shook his head.

"Then believe me now when I tell you that whatever your problems are with this Nazarene, they are nothing compared with the problems Herod Antipas is attempting to work out with the Romans at this very moment. Aretas, the Nabatean king, is threatening war."

"But the law of the Sabbath has been flagrantly broken!" Caiaphas insisted. "Does Antipas care nothing for the feelings of the Sanhedrin or for the priesthood?"

"And does the priesthood, and the Sanhedrin, care nothing about the fact that they have broken their word to Herod Antipas?" asked Chuza.

"What?" came the startled cry from the Pharisees across the room.

"What word has been broken?" Hiram demanded.

Caiaphas quickly got to his feet, avoiding the delegation bearing down on him.

"What word did you give for the Sanhedrin, Caiaphas?" Zepphaniah persisted, following the priest.

When Caiaphas didn't answer, Zepphaniah and Hiram sought a response from Chuza.

Chuza obliged. "The arrest warrant, and Herod's soldiers to serve it, was to be issued when the priesthood and the Sanhedrin took John the Baptizer off Herod's hands. That, of course, was not done," Chuza went on. "And the Baptizer was beheaded. By Antipas. At this very place."

Astonished silence settled heavily in the room.

"Of course, you already know those facts. But what you don't know is that his Excellency believes that it was the place of the Sanhedrin and the priesthood to have disposed of the wilderness preacher."

Hiram walked quickly to Caiaphas, grabbed him by the arm, and swung him about. "Did you agree to such a thing?"

The priest pulled free, his face flaming. "It was the only way to get Herod to agree to let us have his soldiers to find Jesus."

Hiram made a swearing sound. "If we'd had that warrant, we could have arrested the Nazarene ourselves!"

Chuza looked interested. "You have seen the Nazarene?"

"Of course. Only days ago."

"Not only have we seen him, we have spoken with him!" Zepphaniah added.

"Where?"

"In Bethany. At the house of Simon and Lazarus."

"At the house of Simon's wife, you mean," one of the Pharisees said sarcastically.

"Is that the Simon and the Lazarus who are silversmiths?" Chuza quickly asked.

"It is," Zepphaniah said. "Why should that be of interest to you, sir?"

With a careless wave of his hand, Chuza dismissed the question and went to Caiaphas. "Have you had the arrest warrant for Jesus of Nazareth written, as Herod authorized some time ago?"

Caiaphas nodded.

"Then use it, sir," Chuza demanded. "Use it. Herod Antipas will do no more of your killing for you!"

12

By the time the reports about the high priest's disastrous meeting reached the house in Bethany, Mary already had been having a recurrent dream of the mounting danger for Jesus.

For three nights in a row, the dream came to her. The episode was the same in each. It began with a dark cloud moving slowly, relentlessly, across the landscape, obscuring the valleys, veiling the heights of Mount Moriah, where the great Temple was situated. This was followed by a flashing of quickly changing scenes where people were in travail, troubled by heavy cares, reaching out toward Jesus but unable to touch him, and because of that the people seemed to be held by a sadness beyond the deepest of grief. And then the dream would end, unfinished, incomplete, unfulfilled, frightening.

She told Martha about the dream. "I fear for Jesus. The dream is always the same. And it's always so real!"

Martha wanted to calm her sister's fears, but the fear in her own heart so overpowered her that she could only pat Mary's shoulder or hug her for a moment.

She had been afraid ever since the delegation of Pharisees had come to the house seeking Jesus. Next came the news that Herod had ordered Caiaphas to arrest Jesus. There even were rumors that he would be killed. Her fears grew. And now she found Mary's dream to be the most upsetting of all. It was so close. Too close. Too real.

Her fear contrasted harshly with the joy she'd felt over Simon's healing. Fear denied the laughter and satisfaction of serving Jesus and his men when they were guests in the house. Her spirits, which had been so high for so many good things, now were dashed. The contrast brought to mind what Jesus had told his men. "The world hates me, for I bring evidence of the evil that is in the world."

She shuddered at the truth of it, freshly fearful for her friend Jesus. Taking with her all the gloom that was invading her heart, she walked away from her sister and went out from the house.

Her neighbor, Timora, coming along the road toward the house, called to her and waved. A man walked alongside her.

Martha waved back and shielded her eyes with her hand, trying to identify the man. She walked to the gate to greet them.

"Martha, this is Baasha, a friend of my cousin who lives in Jerusalem. He heard about Simon's healing. And he . . ."

Baasha interrupted. "I have come seeking the man who did the healing. Is he here?"

She had never heard Timora mention having a cousin in Jerusalem. She looked at him carefully. He was of medium height and build. There was nothing unusual about his appearance except maybe for the ring he wore on the first finger of his left hand. It was different. But why should that make her feel so undecided about his sincerity, so uncertain of his intentions?

"It was Jesus of Nazareth who healed your husband, was it not?" the man asked.

She nodded, wondering why she felt such reluctance to discuss Jesus with him.

"I have told Baasha all about it," Timora filled in. "But he wishes to hear it from you."

"Or better yet, from your husband himself," Baasha urged. "Is he at home?"

"Simon is at his shop in Jerusalem."

"And Jesus? Where is Jesus?"

Martha shrugged. "He has been gone from this place for many days."

"Did he return to Jerusalem? Or did he go on back up into Galilee?"

Martha shrugged again, feeling ever more uncomfortable about the man. "I think he was planning a trip to Tyre and Sidon."

The man looked perplexed. "Tyre? Sidon?"

She nodded.

Timora turned to Baasha. "That is a very long way from here. Very long way. I have heard that it takes many days to travel to those places. Isn't this true?"

"So you don't expect Jesus to return here?" Baasha asked, ignoring Timora.

Martha shook her head.

"But he has been a guest in your house?"

"Many people are guests in this house," Martha said. "It is the custom of this family to have many guests. Timora will tell you the truth of that, too."

"Where is your husband's shop in Jerusalem?"

A sharp instinct of caution made her hesitate. Yet how could she not tell the location of the shop? It was a very well known shop. Baasha could find it by asking almost anyone in Jerusalem. For that matter, Timora knew its location. Why hadn't Baasha asked her for directions? She cleared her throat and gave a slight cough, hoping the action would be taken as the reason for her hesitation. "The shop is in the Street of Silversmiths near the northern wall of the Temple Mount."

Baasha turned to Timora. "We should go now. There is nothing more to be learned here." He gave a slight bow in Martha's direction and started walking back to Timora's house.

Timora gave a half smile, waved good-bye, and followed him.

At the close of day when Simon and Lazarus returned from the shop, Martha told them of the strange incident and of her concerns about the true identity of Baasha and his intentions about wanting to meet Jesus.

"What did this man look like?" Lazarus asked.

"Let me think. He was of medium height and build. There was nothing really unusual about him . . . except for a ring. He wore it on his first finger, left hand."

"What kind of ring?"

"It was like two golden ropes intertwined with a crescent moon design across the top."

Lazarus and Simon exchanged a look of instant recognition.

"You know the man?"

"We know the ring, my wife!" Simon said. "It is worn by a man named Baasha who is high up in the priesthood and in the Sanhedrin!"

"If he wanted to see Jesus," Lazarus said with a dread certainty, "you can rightly wager it is not for healing!"

Fresh fear clutched at her. "We must go to him. We must warn Jesus."

"Warn him? Don't you think he knows?"

"We must be sure that he does," Martha insisted.

"But Jesus is in Galilee?" Lazarus said. "You women cannot go off up into Galilee by yourselves."

"Then you must go with us."

"I will go," Simon said.

"But the shop. The order of signets for Herod Antipas . . . How can you just up and leave?" Lazarus said.

"I will go," Simon repeated. "Martha is right. Jesus must be warned. He must be made to understand how quickly the danger is growing."

"But Simon, you are needed here. Especially now! Let me go to Galilee and warn him."

Martha went to him and clasped his arms. "My husband, we all know how you feel about Jesus, about how much you feel you owe him. But if you will not let Mary and me make this trip, then let Lazarus go. With all your work for Herod in its final stages, it is you, not Lazarus, who is most needed at the shop."

Simon looked at her for a long moment, and then gave a deep sigh. "Very well. Have your way, Martha. Have your own way."

For Lazarus, finding Jesus in Galilee was not hard. As before, when he and Simon had sought him out, Lazarus once again simply followed the crowds and the directions of villagers who were abuzz with new stories of miracle healings, of preachings of wisdom, and of teachings that helped people understand how to deal with the problems of life.

"Jesus is at Nain," a man in Scythopolis told him.

A shepherd near Nain said, "Jesus went to Magdala three days ago. Ask at the synagogue there."

But when he arrived at Magdala, he found the synagogue closed and the priest away. Nearby, close to the shore of the Sea of Galilee, was an inn. He decided to inquire about Jesus there.

"The Nazarene was here," said the innkeeper. "But by now he should be in Capernaum or Bethsaida or Chorazin."

"Another half-day's journey," Lazarus said, looking about the inn. It was no worse than most he had seen. The weather was turning colder. He was unwilling to sleep out in the open fields this night. "Have you lodging available for me? And a stable and feed for my horse?"

"For a fine-looking animal like that I do. And I can serve you a meal, if you like."

Lazarus agreed. Though the cooking was not to his taste, it warmed him inside.

The following morning, he rode on to Capernaum. Just as he approached a group of fishing boats, he heard a voice calling his name.

He looked around and saw Jesus coming toward him from the shore of the lake. In spite of the coolness of the weather, Jesus wore no cloak as did the other men, who remained at the boats mending the fishing nets. They were all Zebedee's men. None of the twelve were in sight.

"My friend! My friend!" He jumped down from the horse. "At last. I've found you at last."

"Have I been lost?" Jesus laughed, clapping him on the shoulder.

Lazarus joined the laughter, aware of the warmth of friendship Jesus generated. Whenever he was with him, he felt good, confident, joyous. Some indescribable energy came from the Nazarene that was infectious to the spirit.

"Your family?" Jesus asked. "Are they all well?"

"Very well, thanks to you. Simon can do more work than any two men since you healed him. And my sisters both send you their love."

Jesus put his arm around Lazarus's shoulder and began walking toward the house of Zebedee. "That is welcome news."

"But I also bring news that will not be so welcome."

"And that is?"

"You are in danger in Judea." He went on to explain all that had happened—the unrest being created by the Sanhedrin and the priesthood, Herod's order to Caiaphas to arrest and kill Jesus, the strange man that called at the house in Bethany with such pointed questions. "Simon and my sisters sent me to tell you of this danger. To warn you."

Jesus paused and gave him a direct look. "You are a good man, Lazarus. Your family has a generosity of spirit that is rare. I thank you for your warning."

"But you don't seem surprised by it."

"I am not."

"Then you already know how dangerous it would be for you ever to return to Judea?"

Jesus resumed walking toward Zebedee's house.

Lazarus moved alongside of him. The horse followed, reins dangling. "Does that mean you take our warning seriously?"

"I understand the sincerity of your warning."

"Does that mean you will stay out of Judea?"

A peculiar smile crossed Jesus' face. He shook his

head. "The time has not yet come when danger will have its way."

Before Lazarus could protest further or ask for an explanation, they reached the doorway of Zebedee's house and were welcomed by Zebedee and his wife, Salome.

"Come in, friend from Bethany. Sit and rest. Salome will bring you food and drink."

"Where are the others?" Lazarus asked, sitting down at the table where Zebedee indicated.

Jesus sat down across the table from him. "The twelve are away. Scattered to the four winds, I hope. At least, that's where I sent them, two by two, to teach and preach and heal. On their own!"

Salome set a bowl of lentils, a basket of fruit and cheese, and a freshly baked, crusty round of bread in front of Lazarus. "Are you hungry, too, Jesus?" she asked.

"No, little mother. I only need to share the bread and a cup of wine with my friend Lazarus."

Zebedee brought three cups and a flagon of new wine from a sideboard and sat down with them.

Jesus picked up the bread, held it in both hands, and said aloud, "Thank you, Holy Father, for your provisions for us. We break this bread in the spirit of friendship and in your holy presence." He then broke the bread in three equal pieces, handed one to Lazarus, one to Zebedee, and kept the last for himself.

"You should have been here three or four days ago, Lazarus," Zebedee said. "Before Jesus sent those twelve men of his off on their own. We had quite a wonderful experience up in the hills near Magdala."

"What happened?"

Zebedee tapped a gnarled finger against the bread.

"With no bigger a loaf than this, and a couple of small fish, thousands of people were fed right there on the hillside."

Lazarus blinked in astonishment.

"It was Jesus here that did it." He wagged the piece of bread in the air. "A piece of bread no bigger than this, and thousands ate their fill."

Had he not known better, Lazarus would have thought Zebedee was being insolent. But a look of pride and approval filled the old man's face as he turned to look at Jesus. "He has a power like that of no other man I know. And him, born to the sister of my own wife!"

Jesus smiled and spread his hands, palms upward, in a gesture of humility and acceptance. "It is the work of the Holy Father that I do. His abundance overflows for those who believe and who are thankful."

"How did you do it?" Zebedee asked.

"I say again, it is the work of the Holy Father."

Silence settled among them, giving Lazarus his first chance to look around the room. It was large by the standards of most houses in the villages of Galilee. It had two firepits, both large, and both simmering with the heat of freshly placed twigs against the day's coolness. Salome sat near one of them mending a cloak.

Beyond her, on the south wall, a large, shuttered window looked out onto the fishing boats and the Sea of Galilee. On the east side of the room were three curtained sleeping alcoves. An inside ladder led to other sleeping alcoves in a loft.

"When will the twelve return to Capernaum?" Lazarus asked Jesus.

"Within a day or two, I expect. Then we will go up to Jerusalem for the Feast of Dedication."

Astonished, Lazarus glanced at him and was met by a firmly direct gaze.

"Stay here and make the journey back with us."

"Well . . . I . . ."

"Wouldn't you like the rest? It's a long journey, even on horseback, from your house to this. Especially for one not accustomed to so much riding."

Lazarus smiled gratefully. He was tired. Very tired. And though he had tried to ignore them, intermittent spells of nausea were beginning to assail him. He was sure it was the strange cooking at the inn in Magdala. A couple of days' rest would be welcomed.

And, he thought, if he couldn't keep Jesus out of Judea, he might as well be with him. Maybe he could help his twelve men protect him from the Sanhedrin and the priests.

13

IT was early in the morning on the twelfth day of Lazarus's absence from Bethany. Mary walked alone in the garden. No one else in the household was yet up, and she treasured the moments of solitude and the chance to walk at her own pace. "Meditative meandering" Lazarus called it, teasing her gently about never seeming to want to hurry.

She realized how much she had missed him, wondered if he had succeeded in finding Jesus and warning him, hoping he had been able, too, to give Matthew the greeting she had sent, and wishing that he would soon return.

She paused just beyond the great almond tree, savoring the quiet purity of the earliest daylight. The sun was still hidden from full view by the hills of the Judean wilderness in the far distance. Its light filtered across the land in reverential hues of mauve and gray and palest blue. Closer by, just beyond the stone fence that protected the garden, olive trees sentried the hillside. Row upon row, they guarded the slope. Danger of any kind seemed a remote and unreal prospect.

She thought again of her dream. It had not repeated itself since she told Martha about it and since Lazarus went off searching for Jesus to warn him of the hatred building against him in Jerusalem.

She turned back toward the house, the rhythm of her solitude broken, and saw Simon coming toward her. He carried something in his hand.

"Ah, so this is where you are."

She hesitated.

"I have something here that Martha says I must show to you, too." He began to unwrap the small bundle and within a matter of seconds held forth a silver cup for her to inspect.

Even in the uncertain early light, she could see the beauty of it. Its shape was most pleasing and in perfect proportion to the small pedestal upon which it rested. Acanthus leaves and pomegranates adorned the cup in a pattern of infinite detail. At one point the leaves and the pomegranates came together in delicate unity, and beneath them, lying peacefully side by side, were etched in elegant miniature the figures of a lion and a lamb. The work was so beautiful, and had been wrought with such love, that tears came into Mary's eyes. "It's more than a cup, isn't it?" she smiled up at Simon.

He nodded, obviously pleased by her approval. "It is a chalice. A chalice for a king!"

Mary frowned, wiped the tears from her eyes. "You made this for Herod Antipas?"

Simon laughed, loudly and long.

Mary handed the chalice back to him. "You don't

consider Pontius Pilate a king, certainly! Who else of authority is there?"

Simon took the chalice and said gently, "Jesus, my dear Mary. This chalice is for Jesus!"

Of course! She might have known. She looked up at Simon with fresh appreciation. The changes in him since his healing were more than she had expected.

"And the next time Jesus visits this house," Simon went on, "Martha and I want to give a great feast for him and present this to him with all our devotion."

The opportunity for such festivities came much more quickly than anyone in the household at Bethany anticipated. For later on that same day, Jesus, Lazarus, leading his horse, and the twelve came striding up the road from the east.

"We wish not to intrude, my Bethany friends," Jesus said, returning their warm embraces. "My men and I will be going on to celebrate the Feast of Dedication in Jerusalem."

"It is dangerous for you to go to Jerusalem, Jesus." Simon said, casting a doubtful look at Lazarus. "Didn't Lazarus give you the warning?"

"He did. But I will tell you as I have told the others, the time is not yet when danger will have its way with me."

Simon looked at him for a long moment, not grasping the fullness of his meaning, focusing only on the danger that he knew existed for his friend in Jerusalem. "We celebrate the Feast of Dedication in this house, too. Can you make your celebration with us?"

"It would be most unlike us not to expect you and your men to join us," Martha insisted. "At least for one of the meals."

"That we shall do," Jesus agreed. "One meal we shall have with you."

"And when will that be?" she asked.

"On the night before the last Sabbath during the festival," he promised, smiling. "But, before that, I must go up to Jerusalem. I must teach there. There are still many who have not heard the message my Father has sent me to give to them."

After Jesus and his men had gone on to Jerusalem, Simon said to Martha, "When they come back here is the time I wish to give my gift to Jesus."

She agreed. "It will be a perfect time. All the friends we've invited to this celebration meal will be able to see it. They will be so impressed with it."

"Pray that Jesus is impressed with it."

On the appointed day Jesus and his men returned from Jerusalem. They arrived early in the afternoon. Simon had not yet returned from the shop in Jerusalem. Nor had the other guests assembled. Lazarus was in an inner room lying down, resting. Ever since the trip to Galilee, he often had felt ill and had a recurring fever. Only by the sheerest luck had he been able to hide his condition from Martha's sharp eyes.

Preparations for the forthcoming meal were at their most harried. The servants scurried about washing olives and putting them in great baskets, arranging oranges, figs, and dates in bowls. Others were seeing to the cooking of lentils, the baking of bread, and the roasting of two lambs. Still others were bringing in cheeses from the storehouse and unwrapping them. Zoë and two of the men servants brought in flagons of wine.

Martha was everywhere. She supervised everything. No detail was too small to escape her attention.

Mary was trying to be helpful. But her slower pace irritated Martha. Mary knew it, and felt herself a hindrance. With the early arrival of Jesus and his men, she found a reason to be useful as a good hostess, too. She went out into the courtyard taking water for their foot baths. She stayed to serve fruit or wine for their refreshment and to listen as Jesus spoke to his men.

It was here that Martha saw her, seated at Jesus' feet, giving rapt attention to his words.

Resentment stung at Martha. She, too, would like such a privilege. But how could she stop her work to sit at Jesus' feet? If she did, how would any one of the two dozen people expected for the meal actually be fed? Why couldn't Mary be of more help at a time like this, she fumed to herself, staring at her from the doorway.

Jesus looked up, saw her, and recognized that there was some problem. He got up and went to her. "What troubles you, Martha?"

"Mary!" she snapped.

Jesus looked back over his shoulder to where Mary and Matthew were now in conversation. "You don't like it that Matthew finds Mary attractive?"

Martha shook her head. "It is something entirely different."

"What then?"

"She was just sitting there. Doing nothing to be helpful. Just sitting there at your feet as if there were nothing to be done. She knows how hard it is to prepare a large meal. She should be helping me."

Jesus narrowed his eyes, determining the full extent of the resentment and rivalry. "You surprise me, Martha."

"Lord, don't you care that my sister is leaving me to

do all the work for this meal by myself? Tell her to come and help me."

"Martha, Martha. You worry and fret over so many things. And yet so few of the things that you worry over are really needed."

She looked at him in dismay. Of all people, he should understand. Instead he was taking Mary's side. Where was the fairness in that? He obviously did not know what work was involved.

"Very few things are really needed in this life, Martha. Indeed, only one. Mary has chosen that better part."

"What better part?" she asked angrily. "Obviously, Jesus, you've never tried to feed two dozen hungry people all at the same time!"

An odd smile crossed his face.

She hesitated. A recent memory flashed through her mind of the story Lazarus had brought back from Galilee about Jesus feeding five thousand people with a few loaves and fish.

Her anger disappeared. This was her friend Jesus. How could she talk to him this way? A flush of embarrassment rose in her face.

"Let your fears vanish, Martha. They are of Satan. You have no need of them."

She glanced away, embarrassed afresh that he saw her weaknesses so clearly.

"As I said before," Jesus said. "Only one thing is really needed in this life. Mary has chosen that better part. It cannot be taken from her." He turned, went back, and sat down with his men and Mary.

"Why the worried look, my wife?" Simon said, coming in from a side entrance.

She shook her head. "It is nothing."

Simon would not be put off. "Nothing? And with a look like that on your face?"

She relented. "I became angry with Mary, and Jesus thinks I am . . ."

"And Jesus has let you see your resentment and your jealousy for yourself?"

Dismayed, she stared.

Simon gave a gentle laugh. "I've observed that this often is his way. Not just for you, but for all of us."

"I was rude," she admitted grudgingly. "And in all truth, I think Mary does not straggle deliberately or just to irritate me."

"It's just her way," Simon agreed.

"I suppose I owe Jesus an apology."

He came to her and wrapped his arms around her. "You are a good woman, Martha. And I am proud that you are my wife. But come now," he held her at arm's length. "This is to be a festive occasion. This is the night I can give Jesus my present in thanks for his healing. Be joyful, my wife. All will be well."

Their guests began to arrive at that point. Martha and Simon both went to greet them and make them welcome. Throughout the meal all was well. Simon played the part of host with obvious enjoyment. And after the initial shock of having the women join their husbands and the other men at the same table, all the guests seemed to enjoy the occasion, too. They seemed comfortable in the presence of Jesus. They asked many questions and had hearty conversations with his men.

Finally the appropriate time came for Simon to present his gift to Jesus. He rapped at the table for attention.

"My friend Jesus of Nazareth healed me of a loathsome disease, as you all know. I have tried, in many ways, to thank him. I am not sure I have been able to really express what thankfulness I feel. So—"

He paused and turned to Martha, who handed him a small parcel wrapped in a new blue linen cloth. He held up the parcel. "This represents a part of myself. And I give it to Jesus as yet another expression of my deepest gratitude."

With a look of acceptance and understanding, Jesus took the parcel, carefully unwrapped it, and held the chalice high for all to see.

There were gasps of awe and admiration.

"Magnificent."

"Such beauty."

"Great talent, Simon."

Firelight and lamplight shimmered and danced on the chalice.

Jesus handed it to Peter so that it could be passed for each person to see closely. Then he turned to Simon with tears glistening in his eyes. "I thank you for being my friend, Simon. This does represent your great talent and your great heart!" He went to Simon and embraced him.

Martha and Mary hugged each other with joy and, in turn, hugged Lazarus, Simon, and Jesus.

"Forgive me, Lord," Martha whispered to Jesus. "I was rude to you. And we owe you so much."

He looked at her carefully. "You owe me nothing. But you owe yourself the freedom from resentment and jealousy. Be at peace."

Much later, after all the guests had left, and Jesus, his men, and all the household had retired for the night, Martha lay awake thinking of what Jesus had said about her fretting about too many things and about Mary choosing the one thing that was needed. How could she be sure of what Jesus meant? For words of such clarity, how could they be so cryptic?

The next morning Jesus and his men went back into Jerusalem and into the Temple. The Pharisees and members of the Sanhedrin and the priesthood gathered around him in the Portico of Solomon. Suspicion and hostility were clear in their voices. They challenged him. "How much longer are you going to keep us in suspense? Why do you talk in parables? If you are the Christ, tell us openly."

Jesus replied: "I have told you, but you do not believe. The works I do in my Father's name are my witness, but you do not believe, because you are no sheep of mine. The sheep that belong to me listen to my voice."

They scoffed and muttered among themselves, anger growing.

"I know the sheep and they follow me," Jesus went on. "I give them eternal life. They will never be lost. And no one will ever steal them from my hand. The Father is greater than anyone. No one can steal anything from the Father's hand. The Father and I are one."

Some fetched stones to stone him. But Jesus confronted them. "I have shown you many good works from my Father. For which of these are you stoning me?"

They shouted back at him, "We are stoning you not for doing a good work but for blasphemy. Though you are only a man, you claim to be God!"

Jesus answered: "To someone whom the Father has consecrated and sent into the world you say, 'You are blaspheming' because I said, 'I am the Son of God.'

"If I am not doing my Father's work, there is no need to believe me. But if I am doing it, then even if you refuse to believe in me, at least believe in the work I do. Then you will know for certain that the Father is in me and I am in the Father."

They began to shout at him again, scoffing and jeering.

Jesus turned away.

A Pharisee raised his arm to cast a stone.

But John stepped forward, blocked him and shoved him backwards, and at the same time shouted for the Temple guards to come.

The action caught the agitators by surprise.

In the instant of the resulting confusion, Jesus and his men walked away and left the Temple Mount. They returned briefly to the house in Bethany to bid farewell. Then they went back again to the far side of the Jordan to the district where John the Baptizer had first been baptizing, and they stayed there.

The pressures to do something about the man claiming to be the Son of God began to build with alarming speed. The center of the agitation came from three sources—certain members of Herod's court, the priesthood in Jerusalem, and among the Pharisaic members of the Sanhedrin. The clamor grew for vengeance against the man making himself equal to God.

"And those who follow him should be done away with, too," said Hiram the Pharisee as he left the Chamber of Hewn Stone where the Sanhedrin had just finished meeting.

"But thousands follow him," Zepphaniah protested. "To do away with his followers would require mass murder!"

"Then, so it is said, so it is done!"

Joseph of Arimathea, coming out of the chamber behind Zepphaniah and Hiram, overheard, grew pale at the thought, and followed them for a short distance across the wide expanse of pavement toward the Portico of Solomon.

"Where would you start with such a thing?" Zepphaniah asked in an incredulous tone.

Hiram stopped and thought for a moment before turning to his companion. "With Simon and Lazarus. Jesus often stays at their house. Remember?"

"But they are Jews, too," Zepphaniah protested. "It would be killing our own kind!"

Hiram sneered and walked on. Zepphaniah hurried to follow.

Joseph of Arimathea watched them go with a sinking feeling in his heart and a growing resolve to warn the silversmiths in some discreet way. He pondered how that might best be accomplished. Going to their shop would be the most direct way of warning them. But he wasn't sure that was the discreet way to do it. If Hiram was as serious as he sounded, there were many things to be considered for his own safety as well as that of Simon and Lazarus. He leaned on his walking staff for a moment longer considering other possibilities and then straightened as he reached a decision.

The walk to Bethany was not a long one, he told himself. It would do him good. And from all he had heard about Simon's wife, he could find no one better to trust with his message. And he remembered having met her sister with Lazarus on the Temple Mount sometime back. She, too, was known as a trustworthy person, as he recalled, and a woman given to prayer.

When he rapped at the outer gate with his walking staff, Zoë answered.

"My name is Joseph of Arimathea. I am an acquaintance of Simon and Lazarus. Are they at home?"

"No, sir," Zoë responded, bowing to him. "But the mistress, Martha, is here. Please come in."

He followed her through the courtyard and into the main room of the house. Zoë motioned for him to be seated and vanished into another part of the house.

Within a very few moments, Martha appeared. "Sir, we are honored at your presence."

He stood and bowed to her. She seemed a woman of intelligence and somehow much steadier and stronger than the other sister. "I came seeking Simon and Lazarus."

"My husband and brother are at their shop in Jerusalem at this time of day, sir. Have you been there?"

"I felt it would be better to speak with them here, because of the nature of my message."

Martha, even more alert now, asked, "Is it a message you can entrust to me, sir?"

Joseph nodded, began to explain, and then suddenly stopped.

Mary appeared in the doorway, followed by Zoë bearing refreshments.

Martha glanced around. "Oh, come in, Mary. The honorable Joseph of Arimathea has brought us an important message for Simon and Lazarus."

Mary smiled. "I remember meeting you on the Temple Mount. My brother Lazarus was in conversation with you. It is good to see you again, sir."

Zoë placed the refreshments on a small table and once more disappeared into another part of the house.

With a gesture Martha invited Joseph to refresh himself then prompted, "Now, about the message?"

"It has to do with the growing opposition to Jesus. And to his followers."

Mary's eyes widened.

But Martha seemed not to be surprised at the news. "Your message is that Simon and Lazarus are now in danger, as well as Jesus?"

He nodded. "And the two of you. This entire household may well be the target of certain violent-minded men of the Sanhedrin."

Mary sent a troubled look in Martha's direction.

"Is the danger imminent?" Martha asked.

"It well could be."

"You are a kind man to trouble yourself about this," Martha said, once again offering refreshment to him.

He now took a small piece of cheese, washed it down with a cup of new wine, and stood up ready to depart. "Call on me, if you will. Tell Simon and Lazarus to be careful. I shall help as I can."

Martha walked with him to the doorway. "You, too, then are a friend of the Nazarene?"

"There is too much violence in the world, Mistress Martha. Men of peace should avert it whenever they can." He glanced back at Mary and nodded before leaving the house. At the gate he paused and smiled at Martha. "When you tell Simon and Lazarus of this, make them understand the dangers involved."

Her heart came up to her throat, but she did not let her fear show in her face. "I shall do as you ask. We thank you for coming, sir. We are in your debt."

14

BULLA finished counting the bundles containing the signets for Herod Antipas's scribes and turned to Simon. "I make it fifteen bundles with ten signets to each bundle. Does that match your count?"

Simon looked at the marks he had made on the small piece of papyrus and nodded.

"For that much work, we did it in record time, don't you think?" Bulla said.

"Let's hope that Herod Antipas thinks so," Simon answered, motioning for one of the workmen to come and start loading the bundles into a small cart.

"Why should he not?"

Simon shrugged and looked about the shop. "Lazarus," he called out, "We're loading. It's time to leave for the palace now."

There was no response. One of the workmen pointed to the shop's rear exit.

Simon, followed by Bulla, went in that direction and pushed open the wooden door.

Outside, Lazarus, pale and shaking, leaned against the building.

Alarmed, Simon went to him. "What is it, my brother? How can I help you?"

With one hand Lazarus made a feeble gesture. His knees started to buckle.

Simon and Bulla caught him and, supporting him on each side, helped him to a wooden bench behind a neighboring shop.

Sweat beaded his forehead. He began to tremble.

"Bulla, get a cup of water from the shop," Simon ordered, and when Bulla was out of earshot, he leaned close to Lazarus and said, "This is not the first time this has happened to you, is it?"

Lazarus shook his head.

"I will call a physician."

"No!" Lazarus grabbed for his sleeve. "No physician."

"But, my brother—"

"I don't want Martha and Mary to know. They are worrying enough as it is, with all the trouble over Jesus and over our being his friends."

"But Lazarus, we will call the physician to come here. The women need never know."

Bulla returned with the water.

Lazarus sipped at it and with a heavy sigh closed his eyes and leaned back.

"Bulla, go and get the physician Mordecai. Bring him here. Don't alarm our shopworkers, if you can help it. But hurry."

Lazarus opened his eyes, starting to protest.

Simon was adamant. "It will do you no good to object. Bulla has already left."

Lazarus leaned back again.

"How long have you been bothered by these spells?"

"Since I went to Galilee seeking Jesus."

A curious look swept Simon's face. He shook his head. "What an irony."

"How do you mean?"

"I am healed. You are ill."

Lazarus smiled wanly. "I began to feel peculiar after the meal I had at the inn in Magdala. That was before I found Jesus."

"Did you tell him you felt bad?"

Lazarus shook his head. "I didn't feel all that bad then. It was later, much later, after returning home, that the spells increased . . . and . . ." He hesitated and straightened a bit. "You must promise not to tell my sisters about this."

"Well . . . I . . . I . . ."

"You must promise, Simon," Lazarus insisted. "They're already worried about other things, and they'll flutter about until I will have no rest. You must promise."

Before Simon could answer, Bulla returned with Mordecai.

The physician nodded at Simon and went straight to Lazarus, probing him with an inspective eye. He felt Lazarus's forehead with the back of his hand and then grasped his wrist to get the feel of his pulse. "Is his skin always this yellow in tone?" he asked, turning to Simon.

"Why . . . I . . ." Simon said, surprised and looking closely at Lazarus. "No, as a matter of fact, it is not. Why?"

Mordecai now placed his hand on Lazarus's chest, feeling his heartbeat. Then he pressed against the lower right part of the rib cage.

Lazarus gave an involuntary gasp of pain.

Mordecai sat down beside him. "There is some involvement of the liver. That accounts for the yellowish look of your skin, Lazarus."

"What can you do to help him?" Simon asked.

"I will send around a small vial of powder. It is to be taken twice each day, with water. Drink no wine. Eat lightly. Do no work. Rest as much as possible. In two days I will come to see you at your house in Bethany."

"No," Lazarus protested, "I will come to you."

Mordecai looked at him in surprise and glanced toward Simon for an explanation.

"He doesn't want his sisters to know he is ill."

"They already should know that he is not feeling well. Do they not know the color yellow?" He turned again to Lazarus. "I will send the powder to you at once. Take your first dose at once. Agreed?"

Lazarus nodded.

Mordecai stood up, bowed to Simon, and left, following Bulla back through the shop to the street.

"What about the delivery of the signets to Herod?" Lazarus asked.

"Bulla will go with me. You must stay here. You must do as Mordecai tells you."

"I know," Lazarus reluctantly agreed. "But after all our work together on this order, I would so like to see Herod's reception of it."

As it turned out, Lazarus would have found the reception disappointing. Herod Antipas, tetrarch of Judea, Samaria, and Galilee, was not even in the palace when Simon and Bulla arrived with the signets. They were directed to one of the minor officials who served as an aide to Chuza.

"The honorable Chuza is also away from the palace

at this time. I shall inform him that the signets have arrived." He started to turn away.

Simon stopped him. "And the payment for the signets? What about that?"

"You will be paid when the delivery is inventoried."

"No, my friend. That was not the agreement."

The aide gave him a demeaning look. "Agreement or not, I am not authorized to pay you for the signets."

"Then in that case," Simon said in a firm tone, "we are not authorized to leave the signets in your care."

A look of astonishment flashed onto the aide's face. He reddened with quick anger and stepped toward the cart as if to claim it and its load of signets as his own.

But Bulla reached the cart first and was already moving it toward an open doorway that led out into the street.

Simon followed in the posture of a rear guard, keeping good distance between the cart and Chuza's aide. Once Bulla and the cart had cleared the doorway, he carefully shut it in the face of the aide and held onto it, making it impossible for it to be opened from the inside.

The aide began to bang on the door. Loudly he called out for the palace guards.

"Back to the shop?" Bulla asked, looking over his shoulder at Simon, who was straining to hold the door shut.

"No, no! This upstart of an aide will try to follow us and confiscate the signets."

"Where, then? Where shall we go?"

Simon thought for a moment.

On the other side of the door Simon could hear the sound of running feet. "He has aroused the guards."

"Where shall we go?" Bulla repeated.

"To the Arimathean's house. They will never think to look for us there."

"Do you know the Arimathean that well?"

"He is a man of honor. He will help us." He motioned for Bulla to turn and go in the other direction. "Hurry. I can't hold this door much longer."

Simon's assessment of Joseph of Arimathea was right. He was a man of honor. He greeted a breathless Bulla and an angry Simon with all the hospitality and calmness of a longtime friend and colleague, ushered them into his courtyard, and listened to Simon's explanation of what had happened. He instructed a servant to take the cart of signets into a nearby storage area and cover it with palm thatch, while he led his guests into his house.

"We were caught by surprise at the reception we received," Simon said, explaining more fully what had happened. "We have always had good relations with Chuza. I don't understand this change. I notice that my story of what just happened to us does not seem to surprise you. Why is that?"

Joseph rubbed at his beard. "I am not surprised because I know you are friends of Jesus."

"What has that to do with Herod's order for the signets?"

Joseph eyed Simon carefully, as if expecting him to understand the connection between the two facts.

Returning the look, Simon slowly began to realize the meaning of the merchant's words.

"Danger and retaliation and vengeance come in many forms, silversmith," Joseph said, walking to a nearby bench and sitting down. "You have picked up enemies who are deceitful and clever," Joseph said. "Your life will no longer be comfortable in many ways. These new enemies may not want to risk the wrath of the Sanhedrin by physically harming you. But who is to know, or who would care, if they ruined you financially?"

Dismayed, Simon walked to a chair and sat down. Such a thought had never crossed his mind. He had been successful in business all his life. So had Lazarus. They had reputations for quality work at fair prices. Until now there was no reason to think that they would not continue to be successful. With Lazarus being ill, the volume of their business might drop for a time. But that would be temporary, only until Lazarus recovered. The idea that anyone would deliberately attempt to ruin them was unthinkable.

Across the room Bulla had a stricken look on his face.

"We have always had such a good relationship with Chuza," Simon repeated, half to himself, half to the others.

"Perhaps you still do have a good relationship with Chuza. It is important to learn whether or not this is true."

Simon glanced at the merchant sharply. "You mean that he, too, is a friend of Jesus?"

The merchant shook his head. "I did not say that. Chuza is a good businessman. He is also a man who dislikes deceitfulness and violence."

"How do I get around that aide of his?"

"Perhaps I can be of help. I'll try. I will get word to you at your shop. In the meantime, my men will watch over your cart. It will be safe here."

They thanked Joseph and departed, anxious now to check on Lazarus and to take him home to Bethany without arousing the sisters' suspicions about his health.

"That may be harder to do than getting our money

from Herod Antipas," Bulla said with a disheartening laugh.

Simon had been thinking the same thing, and the prospect did not seem a happy one.

Simon and Bulla both were right. There was no way to get Lazarus into the house without attracting the attention of Martha and Mary.

When they arrived at the house in Bethany, Mary was in the garden pruning a small rosebush. The sight of Lazarus leaning heavily on Simon and Bulla sent a shaft of fear through her. Without hesitation she called out for Martha to come quickly.

"Apologies, Lazarus. The women do know you are ill after all."

With Martha in charge Lazarus was quickly settled into his own room. "Now," she said, turning to Simon, "I think we should send for Jesus."

Simon shook his head. "The physician Mordecai has already attended him at the shop. Let's give his potions and his instructions for rest and light eating a chance to work."

"He emphasized that Lazarus should have rest," Bulla put in carefully.

"That won't be difficult. Mary and I will see to it," Martha said, patting Lazarus's hand.

"Rest easy, my brother," Simon said, following Martha and Bulla out of the room.

Once more in the courtyard Martha stopped and searched Simon's face. "What else did the physician Mordecai say about him?"

Simon shrugged. "I told you all."

A fearful look swept her face.

Simon embraced her. "Come, come, woman. Lazarus will soon be better."

She twisted her hands together in a helpless gesture, leaned against him, and began to cry.

The sense of dread that caused Martha to give way to her feelings so completely in front of Simon and Bulla clung to her for the next two days. In her deepest heart she felt she should send a message to Jesus about Lazarus. But she hesitated, wavering between Lazarus's need for healing and her sense of protection toward Jesus. As long as he stayed in Perea beyond Jordan she felt he was relatively safe.

But her sense of dread for Lazarus mounted. And on the morning of the third day, she rose early and, careful not to awaken Simon or Mary, went to find Zoë.

The servant was already awake, moving about with deft quietness readying the fires for the bake ovens. At the sight of her mistress, she stopped and came quickly to her.

"Zoë, who can we send to find Jesus? Who is trustworthy enough to find him and tell him of Lazarus's illness?"

The servant thought for a moment.

"We need Jesus to come and heal Lazarus. I feel it in my deepest heart."

"We could send Mimne," Zoë said. "He is young. But he is smart and he is trustworthy. And he believes in Jesus' healing powers."

"Send him at once."

15

TIME crept.

No word came from Perea.

When Mimne finally did return several days later, he reported that Jesus would be delayed, but that he sent this message to the household: "This sickness will not end in death, but it is for God's glory so that through it the Son of God may be glorified."

But in spite of the message, Lazarus's condition worsened.

On the morning of the sixth day after Mimne had returned, Lazarus died.

Martha held him in her arms, rocking back and forth as she might with a tired child, relinquishing her hold on him only when Mary whispered to her, "He sleeps, my sister. Let us leave him to his rest."

Gently Mary helped Martha to get up, led her outside into the garden so that they might walk together and comfort each other for a time in privacy.

Simon sent servants with the news of the death to all

the neighbors. He sent instructions to close the shop for seven days of mourning. Then he sent Mimne to summon three flute players and six singing women.

Zoë, with the help of Timora and other neighbors, gathered together the spices and wrappings necessary for the burial of Lazarus's body.

Hearts breaking, Martha and Mary led other servants to the family tomb and oversaw its opening, readying the sepulcher to receive their brother's body later that same day.

By the ninth hour all was in readiness for the burial of Lazarus. The procession from the house was led by a group of neighbors serving as lamenters. Amid grieving exclamations and the shrill cries of wailing women, they struck themselves with palms and willow fronds as they processed in front of Lazarus's body on its wooden pallet, which was being borne by Bulla and the workmen from the shop.

The flute players and the singing women followed. Martha and Mary, heavily veiled and clinging to Simon, came next, followed by all the household's servants. Many friends and business associates respectfully stood about the open tomb, heads lowered, eyes downcast.

Joseph of Arimathea, distinguished looking in a blue robe and turban, was among them. Next to him was Chuza, Herod's minister, and Lazarus's friend the Roman centurion Delos Marcus.

The family knelt at the entrance to the tomb and, trembling with sorrow, watched the body on its wooden pallet being placed inside the sepulcher. Bulla and the workmen came out and rolled the huge stone in front of it, sealing it from the world of the living.

Mary began to sob aloud. Martha, in grief-torn silence, comforted her. Simon protectively embraced them both and led them away from the tomb back to the house.

On the fourth day after the burial of Lazarus, Jesus and his twelve men returned to the house in Bethany now so filled with the wailing of mourners and to their friends so filled with grief.

Martha saw them coming and went down the road to meet them.

Mary remained in the house.

"Lord," Martha said to Jesus, "if you had been here, my brother would not have died."

John put his arm around her shoulders, understanding how deeply her faith must run to say such a thing.

"Even now, Lord," she continued, "even now I know that God will grant whatever you ask of him."

Jesus reached for her hand, clasped it in his own. "Your brother will rise again."

"I know," she nodded, "I know he will rise again at the resurrection on the last day."

"I am the resurrection," Jesus said in a quiet, deliberate tone. "Anyone who believes in me, even though that person dies, will live, and whoever lives and believes in me will never die."

Thomas and Matthew cast wondering looks at each other. How could Jesus expect someone to believe his words. Martha so loved her brother. And her brother was dead.

"Do you believe my words?" Jesus asked her.

"Yes, Lord," she answered without hesitation. "I believe that you are the Christ, the Son of God, the one who was to come into this world."

"Where is Mary?" Jesus asked.

"I will go and call her. Rest here in the garden. The house is filled with mourners, as you can hear." She hurried back into the house and said to Mary in a low tone, "The Master is here and wants to see you."

Mary got up quickly to go to him. When the mourners saw her get up and go out, they thought she was going to the tomb to weep there and followed her. As Mary reached Jesus, she threw herself at his feet, and said, "Lord, if you had been here, my brother would not have died."

At the sight of her tears and those of the mourners, Jesus was greatly distressed. With a profound sigh he asked, "Where have you put him?"

Mary said, "Lord, come and see."

Jesus followed her to the tomb sealed by the great stone.

"My brother is here, Lord."

Jesus wept.

Other mourners, coming along behind him, murmured among themselves.

"See how much he loved him."

"He opened the eyes of the blind man."

"Could he not have prevented his friend's death?"

Martha, Simon, and Jesus' men came up and stood watching and waiting.

Jesus turned to his men and said, "Take the stone away."

They started forward to do his bidding.

Martha protested. "Lord, by now the body will smell. This is the fourth day since he died."

With an expression of admonishment, he looked at her. "Have I not told you that if you believe you will see the glory of God?"

His men took the stone away.

Martha stared at the dark opening of the tomb, scarcely daring to breathe, sure of Jesus' power yet unsure of what her eyes would see.

Mary trembled and clutched at Martha's arm.

Jesus lifted up his eyes and said, "Father, I thank you for hearing my prayer. I myself know that you hear me always, but I speak for the sake of all these who are standing around me, so that they may believe it was you who sent me."

A murmur went up among the mourners but died as quickly as it started.

For Jesus now looked directly at the open tomb, staring at it, and in a loud voice cried out, "Lazarus, come out!"

Silence so deep, so intense that not even a bird could be heard settled over all those who were present.

"Lazarus, come out!" Jesus repeated.

And from the tomb, hands and feet bound in the wrappings of death and with a cloth over his face, Lazarus came forward.

To the women Jesus said, "Unbind him, let him go free."

16

THE reaction of Martha, Mary, and Simon to Lazarus's resurrection went from dismay to shock to joy to the rapturous absorption of fulfillment. Their faith in the powers of God, manifested through his son Jesus, now was justified indelibly in their hearts and minds.

For Lazarus himself it was as if he had awakened from a long, deep slumber, refreshed, healed of his bodily affliction, and with a sense of completeness that he'd never known before.

For many of the people who had witnessed Lazarus's resurrection, Jesus became the man to follow, the man to believe in, the man to listen to, the man who could protect them from all troubles—even death itself. But many others did not believe what they saw, claimed it an illusion, a trick of some kind, and they went to the Pharisees to tell them of this latest and most impressive of all Jesus' signs and wonders.

When Hiram and Zepphaniah were told of it, their anger and fears were heightened. Now Zepphaniah agreed with Hiram in what steps must be taken. "We must put Lazarus and Simon out of business," he said, "or else they will forever be a symbol of the Nazarene's powers. We must go directly to Herod and tell him so."

Next they demanded that a meeting of the Sanhedrin be called to deal at once with the heretic Jesus.

"Here is this man working all these signs," said Zepphaniah, "and what action are we taking?"

"If we let him go on in this way everybody will believe in him," said Hiram. "The Romans will come and suppress the Holy Place and our nation."

"We must arrest him now," demanded Zepphaniah, "while he is still at the house of Lazarus in Bethany. We must arrest him now."

But there were others in the Sanhedrin, men of wider vision and of much more conservative attitudes, who argued that to make so much over one man was the greatest of foolishness.

"Why should we give him greater importance than he has?" asked Gamaliel, one of the wisest of the rabbis. "Let him go his way. People will soon forget this so-called resurrection of the silversmith."

A babble of controversy rose up, filling the Chamber of Hewn Stone with argument and conjecture until Caiaphas, the high priest, arose and held his hands high, asking for quiet. Then he spoke to them.

"You do not seem to have grasped the situation at all. You fail to see that it is to your advantage that one man should die for the people, rather than that the whole nation should perish."

They listened more intently.

Caiaphas went on. "I do not speak for my own person, but as high priest. I prophesy that this Jesus must die for the nation, and not only for the nation, but also to gather together into one the scattered children of God."

From that day onward they were determined, as an official body politic, to kill him. "It is the perfect time to do it," Caiaphas said. "Passover will not come until the fifteenth of Nisan. It is now the first of what our Roman friends call February. We will post the notices within the next day and thus meet the requirements of their law and ours. We will find and arrest the Nazarene. And more than that, we will penalize his friends, the two silversmiths."

And so, according to the orders of the high priest Caiaphas, Temple guards posted two notices on the door of the shop of the silversmiths. One notice declared that the Tetrarch Herod Antipas, and all loyal to him, would no longer patronize the shop. Nor would any member of the priesthood. And that any friends of the royal court, or of the priesthood, who continued to buy from the shop would be looked on with great disfavor.

The second notice was published by the Great Sanhedrin and directed against Jesus. It read:

Wanted for Arrest:

JESUS the NAZARENE

He shall be stoned because he has practiced sorcery and enticed Israel to apostasy. Anyone who can say anything in his favor, let him come forward and plead on his behalf. Anyone who knows where he is, let him declare it to the Great Sanhedrin in Jerusalem.

It was Simon who found the notices when he returned to the shop on the day after Lazarus's resurrection. He ripped them from the door, stuffed them into his sash, and hurried back to the house in Bethany.

A great crowd of people, curious to get a glimpse of Lazarus, filled the street. Simon turned aside to avoid them and went through a side gate. In spite of the coolness of the season, five of Jesus' men were in the garden working at various tasks. Matthew sat with Mary under the great almond tree helping her unravel a skein of yarn. Judas of Keriot and Nathanael were counting the coins recently given to them all by grateful followers.

The men hailed Simon.

He motioned for them to follow him into the house, where he found Peter, Andrew, John, and James talking with Jesus, Martha, and Lazarus. He pulled from his sash the two notices and read them aloud.

A gasp escaped from Mary.

Matthew put a comforting arm around her shoulders.

When Simon finished, there was a long moment of silence. Jesus' men looked around at each other, frowning, mutely questioning what they'd heard.

Martha and Lazarus both searched Simon's face for a hint of guidance; but his eyes were on Jesus.

The silence lengthened.

Jesus stirred. "The time comes quickly now."

"Lord?" Martha said.

He turned to her. "One day soon I will be resurrected as I have resurrected your brother."

"You will die?" questioned a startled Peter.

Jesus made no response.

"But, Master, surely . . ."

Jesus silenced him with a gesture of his hand. "I am

the resurrection," he said softly, repeating the words he had spoken to Martha on his arrival back in Bethany. "Anyone who believes in me, even though that person dies, will live." He got up, walked to the door, and looked out at the crowd of curiosity seekers. "I am the resurrection, and the life. Lazarus believes. Lazarus lives."

Mary came to him, looked up into his face, and saw in it a sadness of such depth that her heart cried. "You are suffering, my Lord. Will you not let us help you?"

He turned and smiled at her then looked at the others. "My friends, there is something you must understand. As long as you are my friends, suffering will be part of your lives. You will be persecuted because of your friendship to me, because you believe in me."

He went to Simon and took one of the notices from his hand, read it, and held it high for all to see. "This notice of disfavor by Herod and the priesthood will give you great business difficulties, Simon. All other customers will be afraid to do business with you."

"I know," Simon said in a quiet tone. "It has already begun. A large order of signets for Herod's scribes is still hiding in a friend's shed to save it from confiscation."

"You have but to deny me and all will be well," Jesus told him.

"How can I deny you? You healed me, Lord. I am a fact of your powers."

"As am I," Lazarus said, rising and going to Jesus. "How could either of us deny you?"

Jesus pointed to the crowd standing in the street. "You will be hounded, as I will be one day soon. You will be made to suffer. As I will."

A murmur of dissent rose from the others. Only

Martha and Mary sat silent, not fully understanding the depth of his words, but transfixed by them.

"You must fulfill your destinies as I must fulfill mine," Jesus told them.

Simon narrowed his eyes, calculating his meaning.

"Is that not true of us all?" Lazarus asked.

"It is," Jesus agreed. "But not all have the knowledge of what their destinies are. And even for those who do, sometimes they choose not to fulfill them."

"How can that be?"

Jesus put his arms around the shoulders of Lazarus and Simon, walked with them back toward the others, and sat down. "If, Lazarus, I should say to you that your destiny lies in a direction away from this beloved home of yours, what would be your reaction?"

Lazarus thought for a moment, half-bemused, half-uncertain of Jesus' intention. Finally he said, "Why, I suppose I would resist such an idea. Yes. I would resist the thought of moving from this place. Unless, of course . . . you told me that was the thing I should do. If you told me to do it, it would be different."

Jesus looked at him for a long moment with a penetrating gaze.

"But that's not what you're telling me . . . is it?"

Jesus continued to look at him for another moment.

Astonishment began to fill Lazarus's face. "You are telling me that I should move from this place?"

"No!" Mary exclaimed.

Martha stood up. "Lord, Lord, what are you saying to my brother? How can you mean this?"

"What will I do without him?" Simon asked.

Jesus' men looked at each other in surprise and began to murmur about it.

"Are you telling me I should move from this place, Lord?" Lazarus asked again.

Jesus nodded.

"But why, Lord?"

Jesus turned and pointed out the door toward the curiosity seekers. "You will never be rid of them. Your destiny is thought to be too closely tied with mine in this part of the land. To fulfill your life, you must move. You must move to Joppa."

"Joppa?" Martha said. "But that is clear over on the seacoast. What does Lazarus know of Joppa?"

Jesus continued to look at Lazarus. "Your future is in Joppa, Lazarus. There you can start over in providing for your family, in sharing the good news I have taught you about the new kingdom of love and brotherhood, in fulfilling your destiny."

"But Lord, Martha is right. I know nothing of Joppa."

"As long as you remain here, the curious will gather. The order from Caiaphas and Herod to do no business with you will have its effect. Your whole family will suffer. You will not fulfill your destiny here."

"But Lord . . ." Abruptly Lazarus stopped and straightened. "I am resisting the idea, as I said I would, am I not?"

Jesus smiled.

"And I am resisting you, too."

The room was quiet.

"And yet . . ." Lazarus went on. "It was I who said only moments ago that I would never deny you."

The hush in the room deepened, as if each of the others searched their own hearts to learn the degree to which they, too, might resist or deny Jesus if confronted with an unwanted choice.

Beyond the house in the streets the crowd grew noisier. A complaining sound rose up and brought with it the heavy tread of marching soldiers.

Martha got up quickly, looked out, and as quickly returned to the others. "It is a squad of Temple guards. That man that was here before is leading them."

"What man?" Simon asked, rising and going to the door himself. "Ah, Hiram, the Pharisee." He closed the door and bolted it from the inside.

Jesus' men were all standing now.

"The hospitality of this house is still yours, and for as long as you want it, my Lord," Simon said, returning to Jesus.

"I thank you, Simon. But even in trying to help you, I have brought you trouble." He stood, embraced Martha and Mary, clasped hands with Lazarus and Simon. "You are a close and dear part of me. You are my family. But my men and I must go now."

"Where will you go, my Lord?" Martha asked.

"Over into the district of Ephraim. We have other friends there. And I will teach and preach and heal in that district. I no longer will go about freely among the Jews in Judea."

"Will we ever see you again?" Mary asked.

"I will come again to this house," he nodded, "before the time of Passover."

Simon and Lazarus led Jesus and his men out through the side entrance to the house and down through the farthest part of the garden, which could not be seen from the road in front of the house.

As they disappeared from view, a sharp knock could be heard at the main door to the house. Zoë hurried toward it.

"No, Zoë," Martha ordered. "Mary and I must answer."

Zoë stopped and stepped aside.

Martha unbolted the door and swung it open.

A captain of the Temple guard looked at her grimly. Behind him were six soldiers, off to the right of the squad was a stern and frowning Hiram. "We are looking for Jesus the Nazarene," the captain said.

"And we're looking for the resurrected Lazarus, too!" Hiram prompted with a shout.

The captain seemed to ignore him. "We are looking for Jesus the Nazarene," he repeated. "We are told he is here."

"He is not," Martha returned.

"We will search. Step aside!"

To the surprise of Mary and Zoë, Martha did so without resisting. "Tell the servants not to be afraid," she said to Zoë. "The soldiers are looking for someone who is not here."

The squad followed the captain into the house and began to search.

But when Hiram started to step up onto the threshold, Martha blocked his way. "You are not a member of the Temple guard. You are not allowed in my house. Away with you!" She slammed the door closed against his startled face and against the laughter of the crowd in the road.

By the time the captain and his squad completed their search and were ready to leave the house, Hiram had disappeared from the garden and from the road.

"I hope we won't regret your slamming the door in his face," Mary warned.

"I won't regret it," Martha rejoined. "It felt good."

Much later that same day, after the crowd in the road had dispersed and just as the sun was setting beyond the western crest of the Mount of Olives, other unexpected visitors rapped at the door. Simon opened it to discover the august figures of Joseph of Arimathea and Herod's minister, the honorable Chuza, standing without.

Stammering with surprise, he invited them to come in and introduced them to the family.

Martha scurried off to see that refreshments were brought then returned to join Mary near the firepit.

"We will be brief, Simon," Joseph began. "Chuza has been told of the trouble over the signets. He asked me to bring him here so that he might give you justice in this matter."

Simon nodded.

"As a matter of fact, we came once before only to discover that it was the day of your burial, Lazarus."

"So we obviously could not discuss business with Simon at that time." Chuza said. "Then I was away for a few days traveling with the tetrarch."

"Upon his return he discovered the furor caused among the priesthood, the Sanhedrin, and the royal court over your resurrection, Lazarus." Joseph looked at him directly. "Your resurrection has stirred the fears of many important people. You know that, though, don't you?"

Lazarus gave a grim smile and exchanged a knowing glance with the rest of the family, each thinking of what Jesus had told them only a few hours earlier.

"Fear makes men do peculiar things," Chuza said. "For my own part, I really don't understand it all. But one thing I do understand is that your shop is to be paid for the order of signets just as Lazarus and I originally agreed."

The news was welcome. Simon and Lazarus both nodded with pleasure and bowed to both visitors.

"I have brought the payment with me in gold." Chuza reached into the wide girdle at his waist and pulled forth two money pouches of equal size. He handed one to Simon and one to Lazarus. "So far as future business is concerned, I don't know how much I will be able to help you. That remains to be seen."

Zoë and another servant entered with refreshments, set them on the table, and left.

Martha quickly rose, served the men, and returned to her place beside Mary.

Simon said, "I salute you, Chuza, for your integrity. And Joseph, I thank you for your friendship."

With the departure of their guests, Martha came to Lazarus. "They, too, speak of your future, don't they? And they don't even know of the conversation with Jesus this afternoon."

Lazarus gave a deep sigh. "If these men can see the trouble my new life has already brought, and will bring, to this family of mine, think how much more right is the advice Jesus gave me earlier today."

Mary came to him. "Then you will be doing as our Lord has told you? You will be going to Joppa?"

He looked at her and at Martha and Simon, realizing that he might never see any of these dear, much-loved people again. Within Jesus' advice, there was no easy choice. He pulled Mary to him and, eyes filling with tears, held her close.

17

For the next two months the household in Bethany tried gallantly to adjust itself to the absence of Lazarus.

He had departed for Joppa under cover of darkness on the same night that Jesus had advised him to leave. He took with him a few of his personal tools, a change of clothing, and a letter of introduction to a well-known gem merchant that Joseph of Arimathea had provided for him.

The news of his absence spread quickly among the curiosity seekers in the road at the front of the house. And slowly but surely they gave up the vigil to catch a glimpse of the resurrected man. The onset of early spring rains helped discourage them. Finally the road in front of the house in Bethany was free of crowds entirely.

For members of the household it was a relief to have them gone. Simon returned to the shop in Jerusalem every day. With Bulla's help he set about selling off what he could of the inventory and the equipment. The worst part of closing the shop was telling his employees there was no longer any work for them. "Nor will there be,"

Simon concluded, "unless Herod Antipas should retract his order against anyone doing business with us. And that is not likely."

Martha busied herself with household chores, but Lazarus was always in her thoughts. Sometimes she thought about him so much that his illness, death, and miraculous resurrection seemed unreal, as if none of it had ever happened. But then she would come across a sketch he had done or a piece of his clothing in the household wash, and she would be reminded how real all of that had been. It was as real as his present absence from the house was real. She would shake her head against the turn of fate that had made it all happen, as if the very act itself could bring him back to her.

Mary had similar problems coping with Lazarus's absence. More than ever she sequestered herself with her mending or sewing to meditate and pray for his safety and for his return to Bethany. The gray days of rain added to the burden she felt for him, and she felt an almost equal burden for Jesus.

In her meditations the sense of danger surrounding Jesus was now intense. She had an unshakeable feeling that what he had called "the right time" soon would press against him, and against all their household, as well.

At last the rains gave way to sunlight and to the new life of budding fruit trees and sprouting crops. Ewes lambed and the milk goats gave birth to their kids. Springtime had come to Judea once more. Soon Passover would be celebrated.

"Do you suppose that Jesus and his men will really come for Passover?" Mary asked, as she and Martha walked together through the olive trees, checking on new growth.

A doubtful look crossed her sister's face. "He said he would come. Remember?"

"I remember," Mary said. "But there is still great danger for him. I pray that he doesn't come. Even though I would like to see him again, and . . . the others, too."

"You mean Matthew, don't you?" Martha asked, relieved at a chance to talk about something besides the danger for Jesus.

Mary ducked her head. "I suppose I do."

"Do you love him?" Martha asked, abruptly stopping and facing her.

Mary glanced up at her in surprise.

"Do you love Matthew?"

"I'm not sure. Sometimes I think I do. But then . . ."

"Then what?"

"Sometimes he seems so self-contained that I . . ."

"Self-contained?"

"Or withdrawn. Perhaps that's a better word for how he acts sometimes. Withdrawn."

Martha nodded. "I've noticed that about him."

"When I marry . . . if I ever do . . ." Mary said thoughtfully, "I want a man who lets me share in his feelings and in his thoughts."

"That kind of man is hard to find."

"At first," Mary said, plucking a young leaf from one of the olive trees, "I thought Matthew was that kind of man. Now, I'm not so sure."

"But you'd still like to see him again?"

Mary nodded and gave a small laugh. "Yes. And who knows? Maybe I am in love with him. When I see him again, if he comes again, then I shall know."

Mary did not have long to wait. Six days before the

time for Passover, Jesus and his men did come again to the house in Bethany. But her enjoyment at seeing Matthew was overshadowed by the unexpected arrival of Lazarus, as well.

"I had to come," Lazarus said, whirling his astonished sisters about in a dance of joy. "The fact that Jesus and his men are here makes it all the more perfect."

By the time Simon returned from the shop that day, Martha had started preparations for a dinner. Timora, the neighbor, came to help, and Mimne was asked to bring his lyre into the room and play for the guests. Martha supervised all the work and waited on the guests herself.

Mary brought in a pound of very costly ointment, pure nard. Its precious scent filled the house, adding to the feelings of joy and celebration. She went to where Jesus sat, looked up at him as if asking his permission, and anointed his feet with the ointment.

He nodded and smiled at her.

Others sat up in astonishment, watching the act.

Judas of Keriot scurried to Jesus and said to him in a low tone, "This is a waste, my Lord. Why is this ointment not sold for three hundred denarii and the money given to the poor?"

John, sitting next to Jesus, overheard, and turned to Judas. "You don't care about the poor. If you did, you would give from our common fund instead of . . ."

Jesus held up a restraining hand.

John said nothing more.

Jesus looked at Judas. "You will have the poor with you always. You will not always have me. Leave the woman alone. Let her keep what remains of the ointment for the day of my burial."

Resentment showing in his face, Judas backed away and returned to his place at the foot of the table.

Mary finished the anointing, set aside the ointment, and began to dry Jesus' feet with her hair.

When the meal was almost finished and fresh torches were brought in to replace those that had burned low, Martha noticed that Judas was not present. Neither was Timora.

She thought nothing more about it until three days later when a large number of Jews came from Jerusalem seeking Jesus and Lazarus. The curiosity seekers were back, and she suspected that Timora had spread the word.

At the back of the crowd she thought she saw Judas near a man wearing a red and white turban and robe like those worn by Hiram, the Pharisee. But she couldn't be sure, for when she turned to take a second look, he was obscured by what she could clearly identify as a squad of Temple guards.

Suspicion turned to alarm. Martha closed the door, grabbed a shawl, and pulled it close about her. She left the house by a side door to mingle with the crowd and listen to what they were saying. And what they were saying surprised her.

"I didn't just come to see Jesus," said a tall man in a white linen tunic. "I came to see the resurrected man, Lazarus."

Another said, "I, too, want to see Lazarus. I already believe in Jesus. So do most of my friends."

"It was because of Lazarus that I came to believe in Jesus," said yet another man.

"If Jesus can raise a man from the dead, he surely must have the power of God."

Three others nodded agreement and one said, "Surely he must be the Son of God."

All these expressions were of an attitude Martha had not expected. But when she came near the man in the red and white turban and robes, and those who were standing with him next to the Temple guards, she heard a different expression.

"Now do you believe me, Caiaphas?" asked Hiram, the Pharisee. "Now do you understand that we must kill Lazarus as well as Jesus?"

Alarm turned to fear. Kill? Kill Lazarus? Kill Jesus? They must be warned. With cautious haste she slipped through the crowd back toward the house to find them.

They were talking together at the back of the house in a sheltered spot that Mary often used for her meditations.

Martha came upon them breathless and frightened. As she reported what she had heard, the expression on Lazarus's face turned from one of curiosity to one of genuine alarm. Jesus, by contrast, did not seem at all surprised. "It is that the prophecy will be fulfilled where I am concerned," he said in a resigned tone.

Mary and Simon appeared at the edge of the sheltered area, followed by Matthew and John.

Jesus held out his hand, beckoning them to come closer. "The time has come when the prophecy must be fulfilled."

"But, my friend . . ." Lazarus protested. "It is not too late for you to flee."

"I cannot flee. This is a commitment I must fulfill for my Father," he said, as if patiently explaining it all to a child.

Martha looked at Lazarus, wondering if he felt the

same weight of sadness as she did. But he was staring at Jesus as if he thought him mad.

"It is you, Lazarus, who must flee," Jesus said. "Only now you must take Martha and Mary and Simon with you."

Matthew cast a distraught look toward Mary.

"You must do as I say," Jesus said in a commanding way. "This time you have no choice. You must close up this house, take the family to Joppa, and as quickly as possible arrange to travel on to Cyprus."

"Cyprus?" They said it as a chorus, united in amazement, stunned at his words, dismayed at the very idea.

"But this house—this land—has belonged to my family since the days of the Roman conqueror Ptolemy," Martha asserted. "I cannot imagine not living here."

"You must imagine it, Martha," Jesus said bluntly. "If you wish to save your brother's life, you must imagine it."

Mary began to weep. Matthew tried to console her, but she ran to Martha and clung to her.

Martha and Simon looked at each other.

Lazarus stood up. "Why can't I just leave? If I am the one they want to kill, why does the whole family have to suffer."

"Because they are your family," Jesus said. "This family must go to a place where neither the priesthood, the Sanhedrin, nor the authority of Herod Antipas can legally touch it. Cyprus is such a place."

They all looked at Jesus, wondering whether or not he would change his advice, knowing he would not, knowing also that they had no honest right to question his wisdom. He had healed Simon. He had given Martha a peace of mind and contentment that her perfectionism never before had allowed her to experience. He had appreciated Mary's quiet ways so that her confidence was bolstered. And he had raised Lazarus from the dead. How could they question his wisdom? How could they refuse to do as he now advised?

"We will never see you again, will we?" Mary said, wiping at her tears.

He smiled at her. "I will be with you always."

18

"TELL this place farewell with particular af-
fection," Martha instructed Lazarus and Mary, as they
stood in the darkness of the road looking back at their
beloved home. "We were born here. We have lived here
all our lives, buried our parents and grandparents from
this house."

"And even buried me from this house," Lazarus said
in a peculiar tone.

"We have seen miracles done in and for this house
like none other," Simon said.

"Yes, praise be," Martha said, grasping Simon's arm
and giving it an affectionate squeeze.

"And our Lord has been a guest in this house many
times," Mary said quietly.

"He, to whom we owe all, will always be a part of this
place, as will we," Martha agreed.

"Come," Lazarus said. "We must go before Timora's
curiosity brings her out into the street in darkness to
discover our departure."

Zoë waved to them from just inside the gate and wiped

at her eyes with a corner of her apron. All the other servants had been ordered to stay indoors so that the departure would be unnoticed. Jesus and his men, who were remaining in the house overnight, did likewise. On the next day they would go into Jerusalem for Passover.

In the days to come Zoë had been instructed to tell everyone that the family had gone into Jerusalem to celebrate the Passover.

In actuality Zoë, Mimne, and Bulla would join the family in a few days at the port in Joppa and sail to the island of Cyprus with them. Joseph of Arimathea had arranged for their transportation and beyond that had agreed to care for the house in Bethany and its lands until a permanent overseer could be hired to care for it.

"We will need the income from the gardens and the orchards, I expect," Simon had told Joseph. "You and your people will of course be recompensed for your trouble. Again, we are indebted to you for your kindness."

Hearts filled to overflowing with strange emotions, they waved back to Zoë and the house and made their way in silence up the slope of the Mount of Olives. It was two days before Passover. Only the extreme need of their personal situation would have made them travel at this particular season. But Jesus had insisted that they not delay in getting to Joppa.

They arrived on its outskirts two days later. Passover Sabbath would begin at sunset. But they had walked steadily for two days to reach this point, and now they rested and looked at the city and the Great Sea beyond. The sea was cobalt in color, and spread endlessly across the horizon. No matter the direction they looked from south to north and back again, all they could see was water. It filled the world beyond Joppa.

"I have never seen so much water," Mary exclaimed.

Lazarus and Simon agreed. "Even the Sea of Galilee shows its opposite shoreline," Simon said.

"Where is Cyprus?" the practical Martha asked.

Simon went to her, put his arm around her, turned her a bit, and with the other arm pointed west northwest. "In that direction beyond the horizon."

In a sudden surge of emotion, she turned to him. "Will we ever see our house in Bethany again?" Tears sprang to her eyes, and she looked away, trying to hide them.

Simon pulled her close and held her.

"It will be all right, my wife," he reassured her. "Jesus would not have told us to do this if it was wrong."

She pulled out a linen square and wiped her eyes dry.

"Come," Lazarus urged. "We'll soon be at our destination." He set off again, leading them down a small hill toward the gates of the city and to the house of the gem merchant who was the friend of Joseph of Arimathea. Zoë, Mimne, and Bulla were to meet them there as soon as they could. They were coming by a different route: through Jerusalem itself, to Emmaus, and on to Joppa.

"If they don't get here before Sabbath begins, we should not expect to see them for at least another day," an impatient Martha said. "You know that Zoë and Bulla, good Jews that they are, will not travel on the Sabbath."

"Patience, my sister," Lazarus said. "You'll not be bored. There is a lot to see in Joppa."

And indeed there was. The women went to the bazaar to look at all the merchandise brought to Joppa from the lands beyond the Great Sea. Simon and Lazarus visited with their host; and then all five of them walked together along the seashore in fine, clear weather.

Their host pointed out various important sites in the

city. The companionship was easy, the conversation interesting, and the weather remained clear and fine until about the ninth hour. Then, as if from nowhere, the skies darkened with a dread darkness.

Mary gave a sudden shiver.

Martha noticed the change and wondered at it.

Off to the southeast, in the direction of Jerusalem, lightning cut through the somberness with savage intensity and brought a command of thunder that rolled from horizon to horizon, as if the voice of God was shouting to all humanity.

Mary shivered uncontrollably and then gave an embarrassed laugh when she realized that all the rest were looking at her.

"Perhaps it is time to go back to the house," the gem merchant said. "Sometimes when the vastness of the sea matches the vastness of the heavens, it is a troubling experience."

They turned back toward their host's house to join with him in celebration of a Passover Sabbath supper. Out across the Great Sea the dark clouds suddenly parted. The sun, drifting on its sunset course, painted sky and sea vermilion, charcoal, cobalt, pink, and vermilion again.

The following day, early in the morning, a rapid knocking at the door of the gem merchant's house brought every person awake and to their feet. Lazarus went with their host to open the door.

Zoë, Bulla, and Mimne had arrived.

"You look as if you've traveled all night," Lazarus exclaimed.

"We have," said Bulla in a weary voice. "We dared not linger in Jerusalem. Even though we broke the Sabbath, we dared not linger."

Martha came up behind Lazarus, took one look at the

strained expression on Zoë's face, and rushed toward her in concern. "Zoë! Are you ill?"

"Oh, mistress. My mistress," the servant cried. "They have killed him! They have crucified our Lord!"

A stab of stark horror went through her.

Lazarus paled, looking more lifeless than on the day he was entombed in Bethany.

Simon's face froze into a look of unbelieving anger.

Mary fell to her knees, covered her face with her hands, and began to sob.

Bulla and Mimne came into the house, stood beside Lazarus and Simon, and began to murmur the prayer that Jesus had taught them.

"Our Father, who is in heaven,
Hallowed be your name.
Your kingdom come, Your will be done
On earth as it is done in heaven.
Give us today our daily bread,
And forgive us our debts,
As we forgive our debtors.
Lead us not into temptation,
But deliver us from evil.
For yours is the kingdom, and the power,
and the glory, forever."

Those who mourned stood together without moving for many moments after the softly prayerful voices of Bulla and Mimne finished. There was no sound now except that which came from broken hearts—the sounds of those too moved to speak, too hurt to give expression to the depth of their sadness, too torn even to wonder if their spirits would ever again soar with the joy and peace of having known such a person as the man called Jesus of Nazareth.

The gem merchant moved carefully around the grief-stricken group and motioned for one of his servants to bring wine and fruit, bread and cheese.

"We were there," Zoë said, looking up at Martha. "We saw them put a crown of thorns on his head, press it into his flesh until the blood ran down onto his face. We saw . . ."

Martha took the devastated Zoë into her arms. "Don't think about it."

"I must think about it, my mistress. I must. I will forever see him nailed to that awful cross. Above his head they placed a sign that read 'King of the Jews'!"

"He never acted like a king," Mimne said slowly. "He was our friend."

"Who claimed his body?" Simon asked Bulla.

"The Arimathean. And another member of the Sanhedrin, a man named Nicodemus."

Simon smiled. "That would be Nicodemus the banker." He scratched at his head. "What an irony that a merchant and banker should claim the body of a wandering preacher, who just happens to be the Son of God."

A look of peculiar interest filtered into the eyes of the gem merchant. He came to Simon. "You believe that?"

"I do."

He turned to Martha. "And you and your sister and brother? You all believe that this man you mourn is the Son of God?"

The others joined with Martha and Simon in affirming their belief.

"But why would you believe such a thing?" the gem merchant pressed.

"Because he healed me," Simon said.

"And because he raised me from the dead," Lazarus added. "Powers of that kind are of God."

"No one but a Son of God could share them and use them as Jesus did," Mary spoke up suddenly, tears of mourning still staining her face.

"And more than that," Martha said. "My sister here saw the Spirit of God descend on Jesus when he was baptized by John the Baptizer in the River Jordan."

They all looked at Martha, surprised to hear her confirm what they all thought she had for so long been skeptical of.

"You believe me!" Mary exclaimed.

"For quite a long time," Martha answered with a twinge of embarrassment.

For a long moment the two sisters looked at each other in a new bond of understanding and love.

The moment was broken by another question from the gem merchant. "If you are a good Jew, do you believe that God is forever? Eternal? That God is God, without beginning, without end?"

Simon and Lazarus looked at each other, then at their sisters, and the others. "Of course we believe that God is forever. Forever alive!"

The gem merchant walked up very close to Martha and looked at her directly. "If that is so, then why do you let all this family of yours so mourn for the Son of God?"

She backed away, as if to get a better look at him, as if to improve her perspective, as if to fathom his full intent.

The gem merchant followed her. "If you believe that

God is eternal, why should you not believe that his son, too, is eternal?"

"But . . . but . . ." stammered Zoë, "they crucified him. He died on that awful cross."

The gem merchant said, "But you have forgotten the most important thing. The better part."

They all stared at him. For Martha his use of the words *the better part* had special meaning. They were the very words Jesus had spoken to her when she felt such resentment toward Mary. She stared at the gem merchant, like all the rest, wondering what he meant.

"What you are forgetting is that which was written by the prophets long ago. 'On the third day, he shall rise.'" He looked at each one of them carefully. "On the third day, he shall rise," he repeated. "The third day is to-morrow."

Martha felt thunderstruck.

The others looked as if they felt the same.

Jesus alive as Lazarus was alive!

Simon finally turned to her. "What was it Jesus said to you about the resurrection of Lazarus?"

"That he himself would be resurrected as he had resurrected Lazarus." She walked away from the others, went to the door, and looked out, beginning to understand what Jesus meant by the better part and how important it was to tell others about him and about the ongoing of life he represented.

She turned and looked at the others, loving them all more than ever.

Especially Mary. Loving, gentle Mary who first recognized Jesus for what he was and who he is.

It would not be at all surprising, Martha decided, if

Mary had yet another vision of his Holy Spirit. It would come to her, as it had come before, as a gift to her own gentle and loving spirit. And she, Martha, would be glad that it had come to Mary.